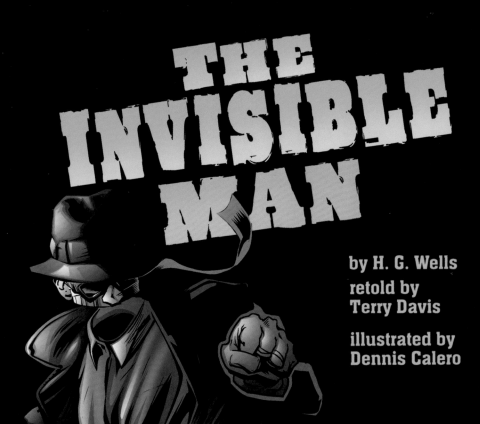

THE INVISIBLE MAN

by H. G. Wells

retold by
Terry Davis

illustrated by
Dennis Calero

Librarian Reviewer
Katharine Kan
Graphic novel reviewer and Library Consultant, Panama City, FL
MLS in Library and Information Studies, University of Hawaii at Manoa, HI

Reading Consultant
Elizabeth Stedem
Educator/Consultant, Colorado Springs, CO
MA in Elementary Education, University of Denver, CO

STONE ARCH BOOKS
MINNEAPOLIS   SAN DIEGO

Graphic Revolve is published by Stone Arch Books,
151 Good Counsel Drive, P.O. Box 669,
Mankato, Minnesota 56002.
www.stonearchbooks.com

Library of Congress Cataloging-in-Publication Data
Davis, Terry.
The Invisible Man / H.G. Wells; retold by Terry Davis; illustrated by Dennis Calero.
      p. cm. — (Graphic Revolve)
      ISBN-13: 978-1-59889-831-6 (library binding)
      ISBN-10: 1-59889-831-0 (library binding)
      ISBN-13: 978-1-59889-887-3 (paperback)
      ISBN-10: 1-59889-887-6 (paperback)
      1. Graphic novels. I. Calero, Dennis. II. Wells, H. G. (Herbert George), 1866–1946.
Invisible Man. III. Title.
PN6727.D36I58 2008
741.5'973—dc22   2007006200

Summary: Late one night, a man covered in bandages wanders into a village. The villagers
soon grow suspicious of the stranger. When the villagers attempt to arrest him, the
stranger suddenly reveals his secret — he is invisible!

Art Director: Heather Kindseth
Graphic Designer: Brann Garvey

1 2 3 4 5 6 12 11 10 09 08 07

Printed in the United States of America

TABLE OF CONTENTS

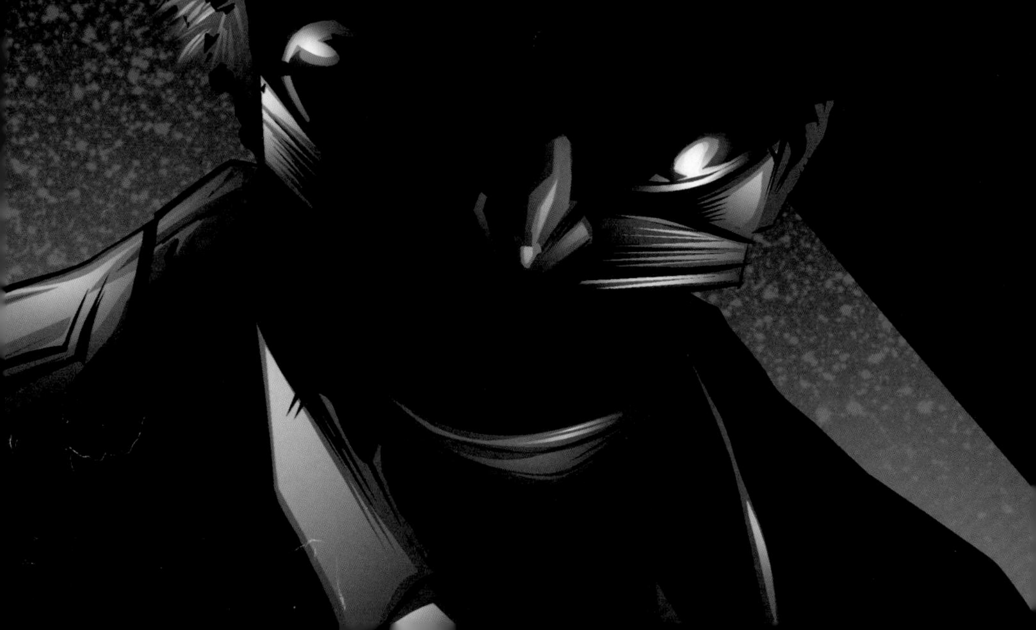

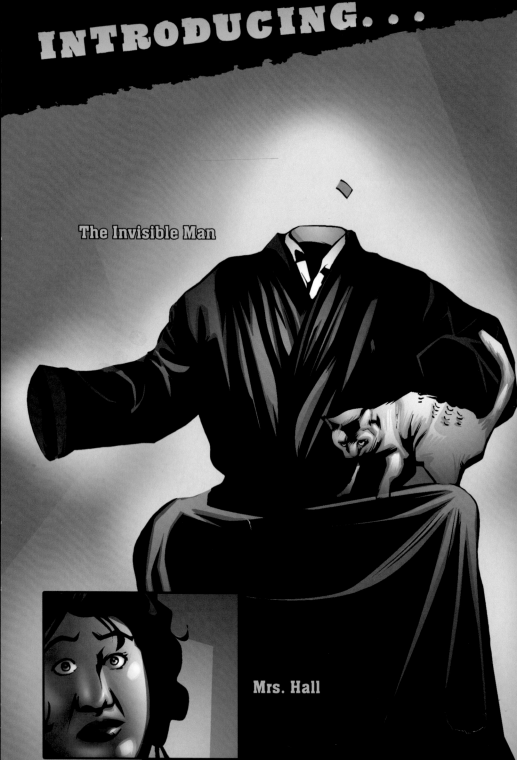

The Invisible Man

Mrs. Hall

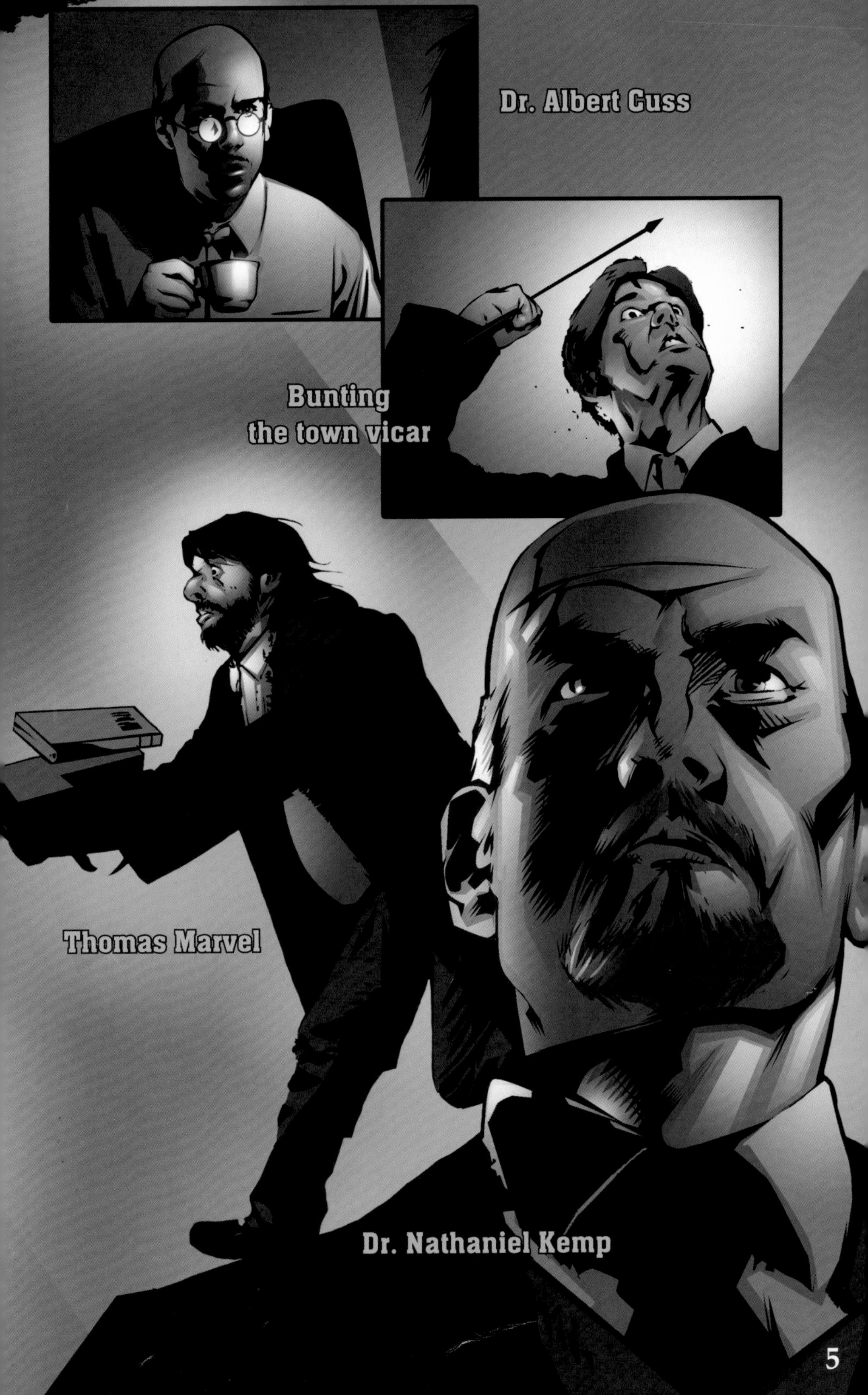
Dr. Albert Cuss
Bunting
the town vicar
Thomas Marvel
Dr. Nathaniel Kemp

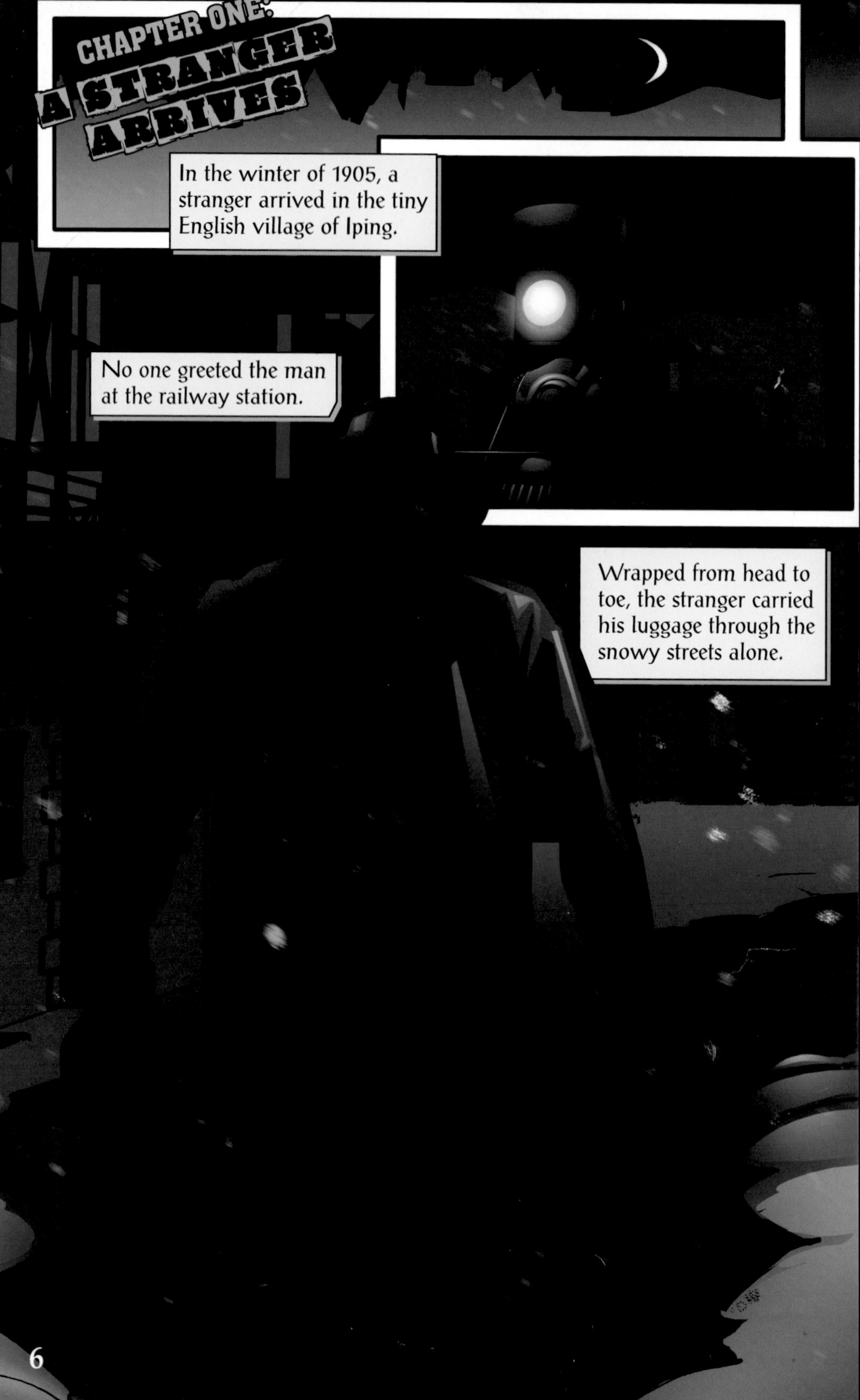
CHAPTER ONE:
A STRANGER ARRIVES
In the winter of 1905, a stranger arrived in the tiny English village of Iping.
No one greeted the man at the railway station.
Wrapped from head to toe, the stranger carried his luggage through the snowy streets alone.

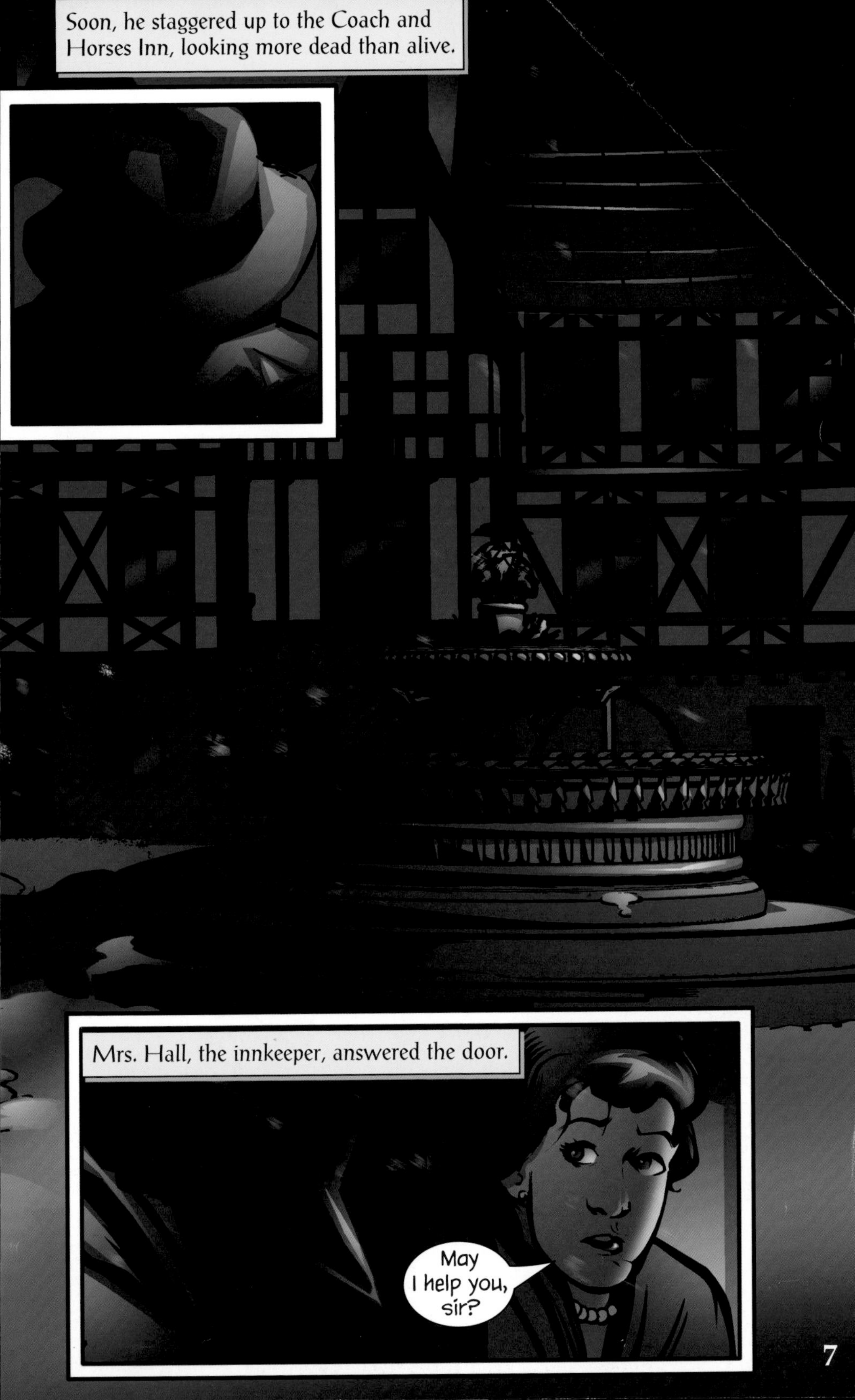
Soon, he staggered up to the Coach and Horses Inn, looking more dead than alive.
Mrs. Hall, the innkeeper, answered the door.
May I help you, sir?

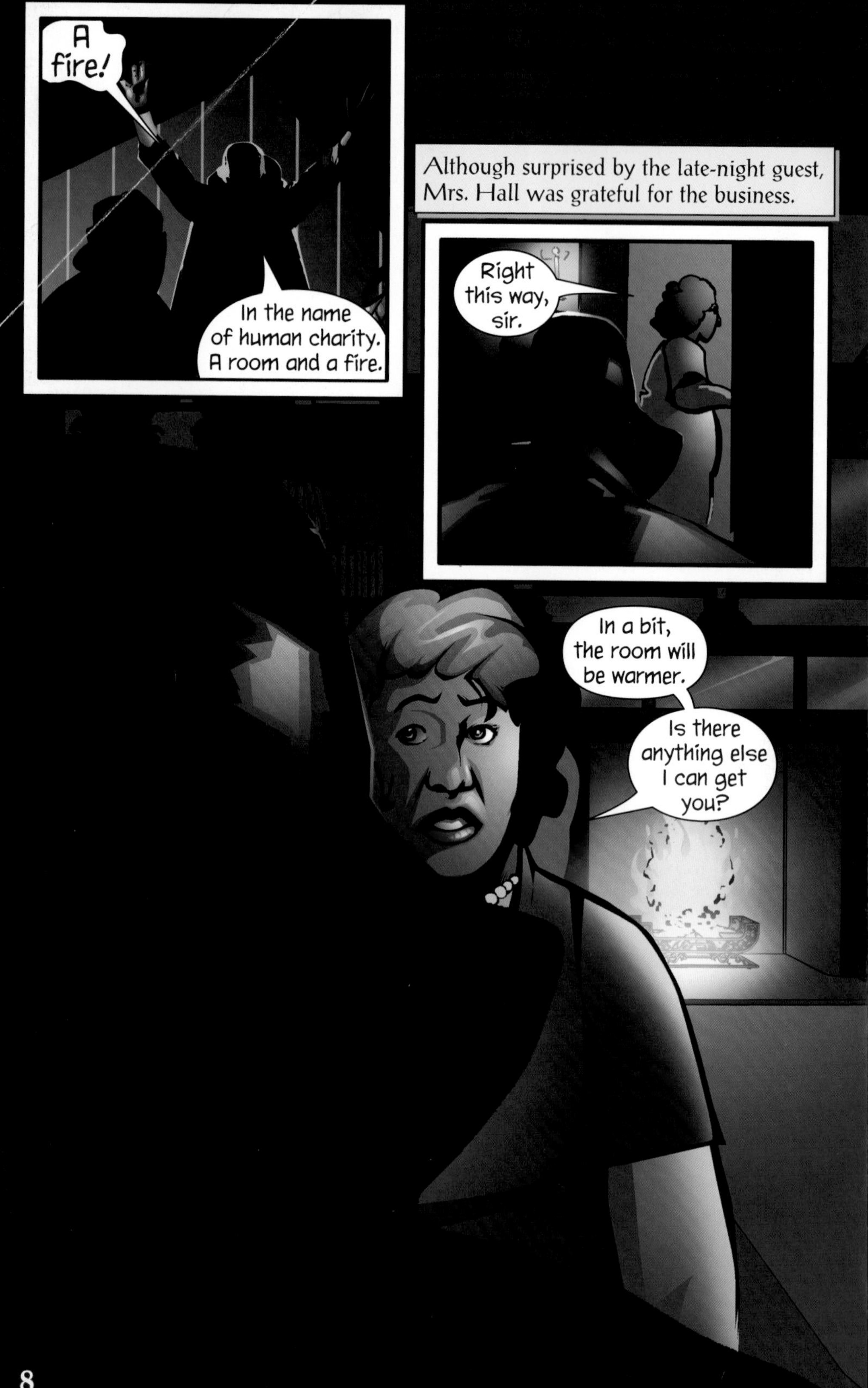
A fire!
In the name of human charity. A room and a fire.
Although surprised by the late-night guest, Mrs. Hall was grateful for the business.
Right this way, sir.
In a bit, the room will be warmer.
Is there anything else I can get you?

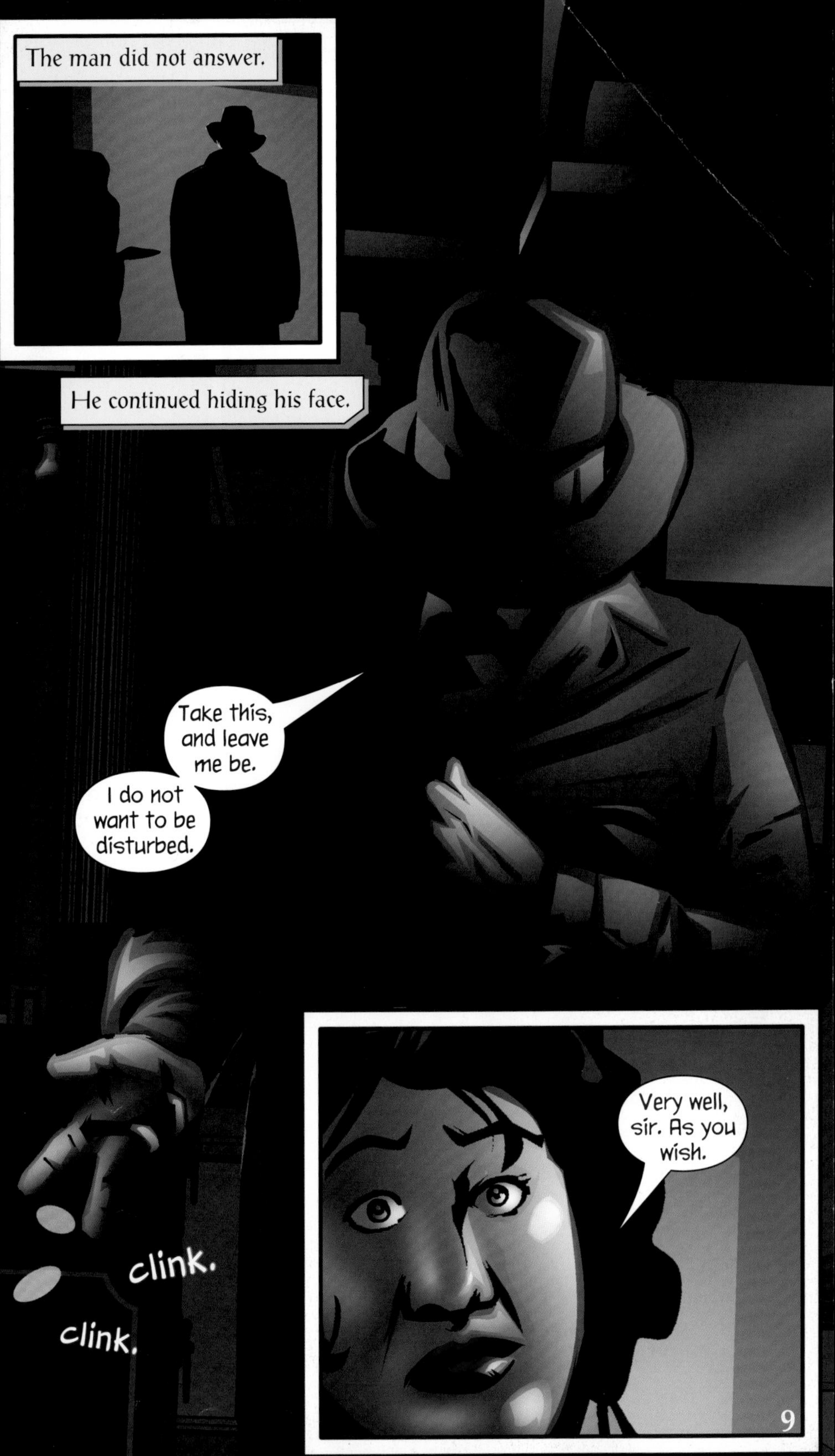
The man did not answer.
He continued hiding his face.
Take this, and leave me be.
I do not want to be disturbed.
clink.
clink.
Very well, sir. As you wish.

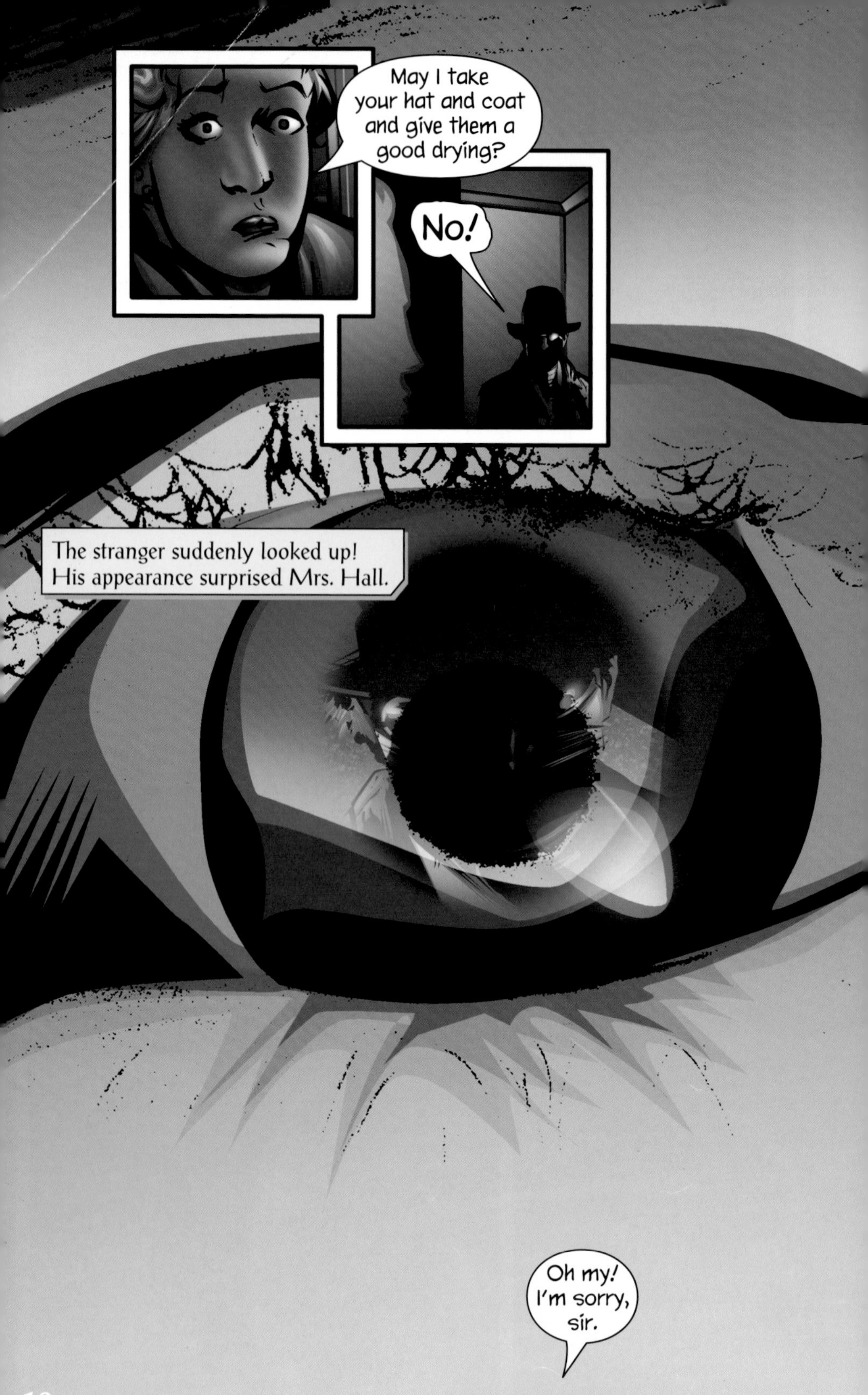
May I take your hat and coat and give them a good drying?
No!
The stranger suddenly looked up! His appearance surprised Mrs. Hall.
Oh my! I'm sorry, sir.

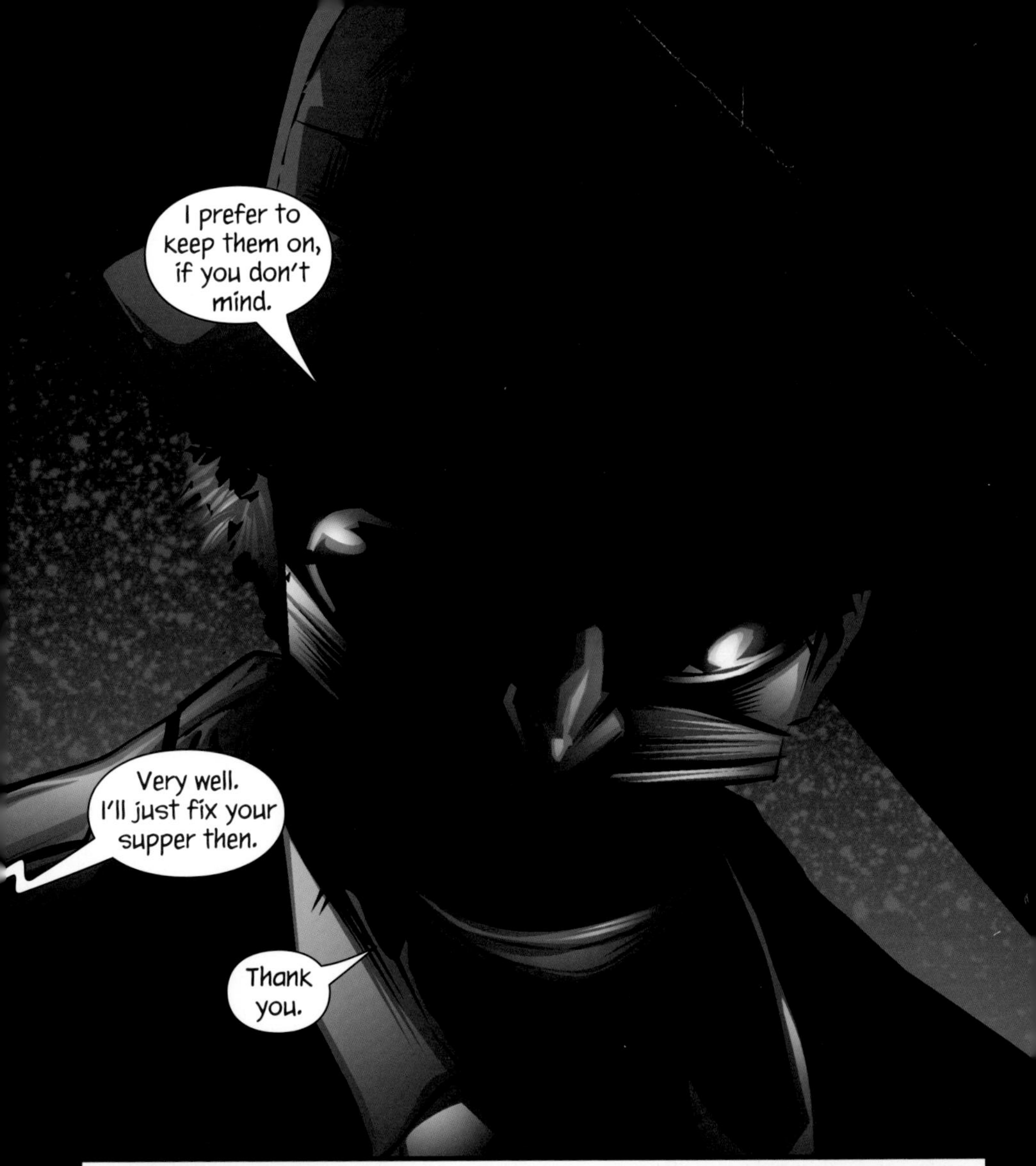
I prefer to keep them on, if you don't mind.
Very well. I'll just fix your supper then.
Thank you.

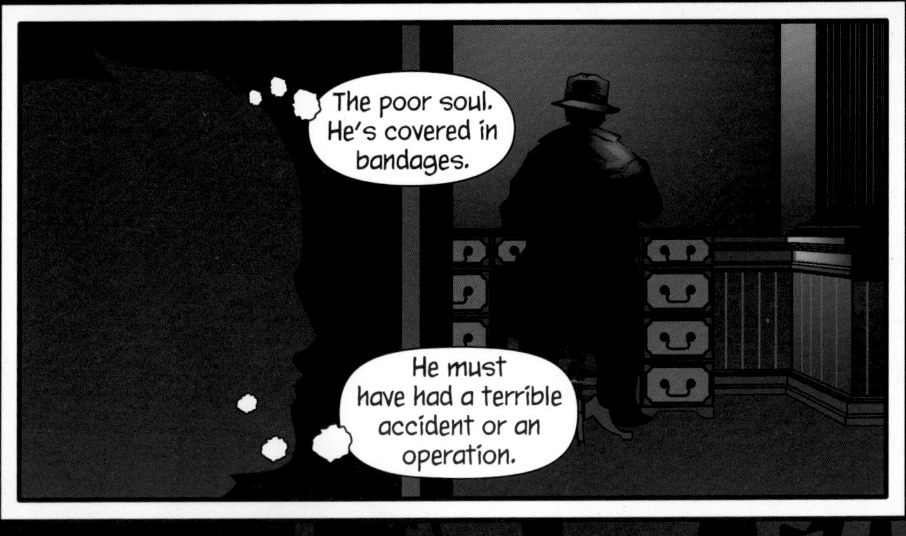
The poor soul. He's covered in bandages.
He must have had a terrible accident or an operation.

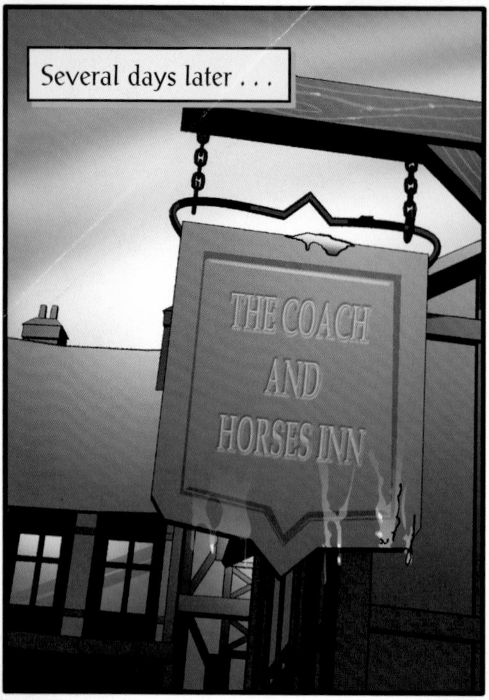
Several days later . . .
THE COACH AND HORSES INN

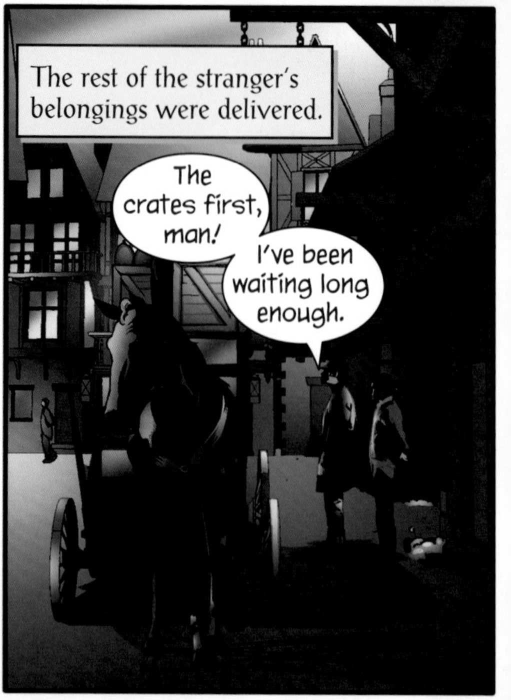
The rest of the stranger's belongings were delivered.
The crates first, man!
I've been waiting long enough.

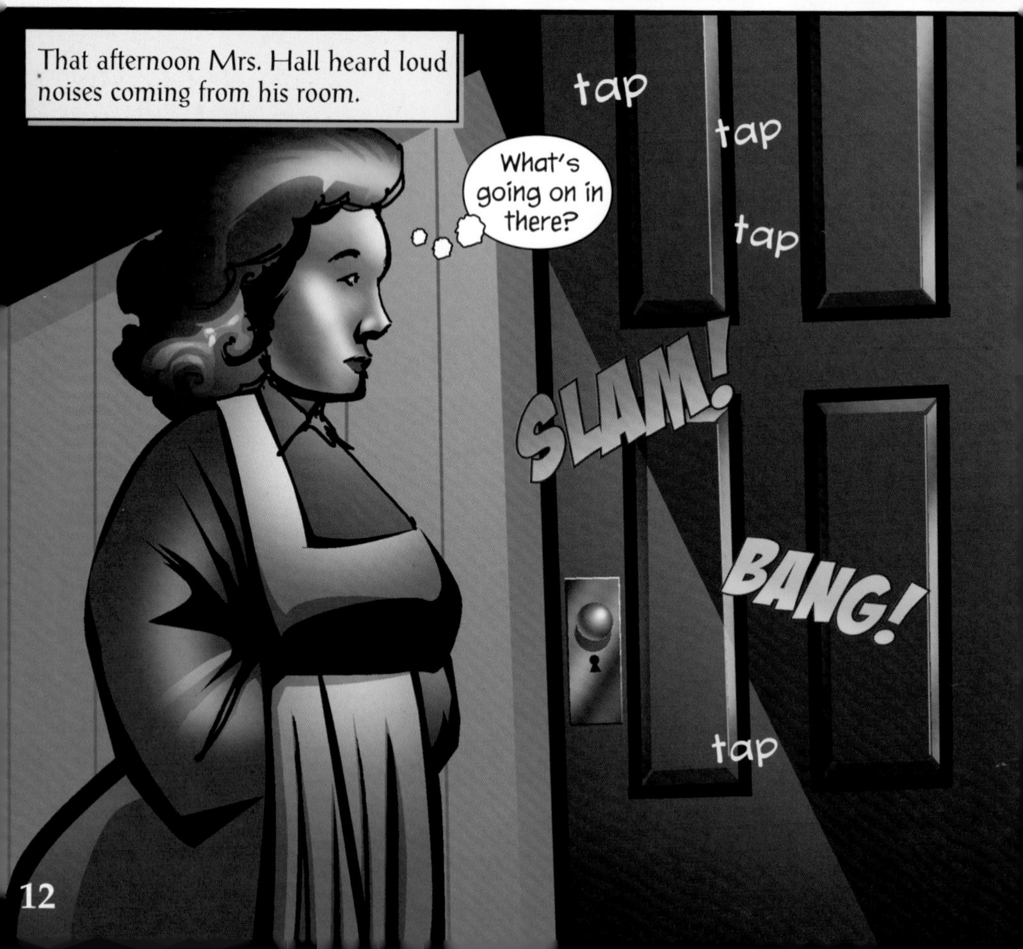
That afternoon Mrs. Hall heard loud noises coming from his room.
What's going on in there?
tap
tap
tap
SLAM!
BANG!
tap

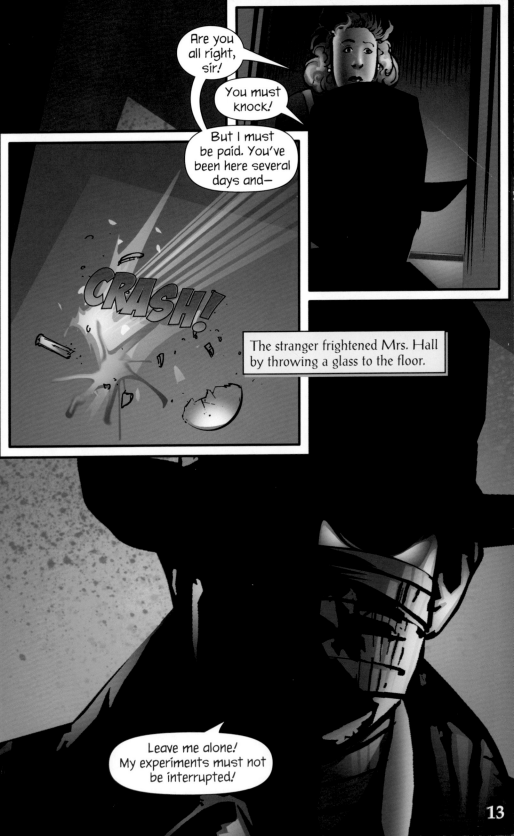

Are you all right, sir!

You must knock!

But I must be paid. You've been here several days and—

CRASH!

The stranger frightened Mrs. Hall by throwing a glass to the floor.

Leave me alone! My experiments must not be interrupted!

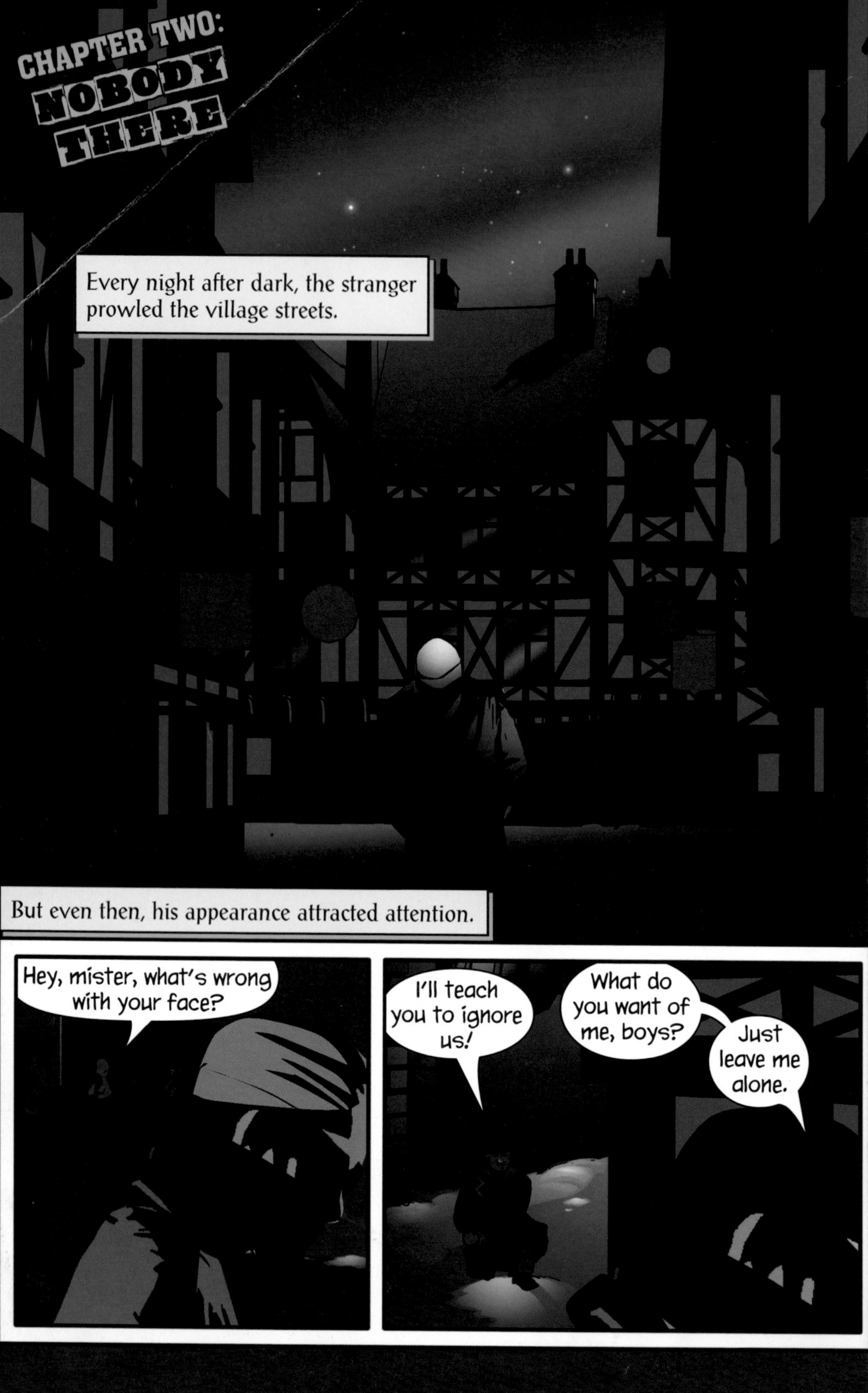
CHAPTER TWO:
NOBODY THERE
Every night after dark, the stranger prowled the village streets.
But even then, his appearance attracted attention.
Hey, mister, what's wrong with your face?
I'll teach you to ignore us!
What do you want of me, boys?
Just leave me alone.

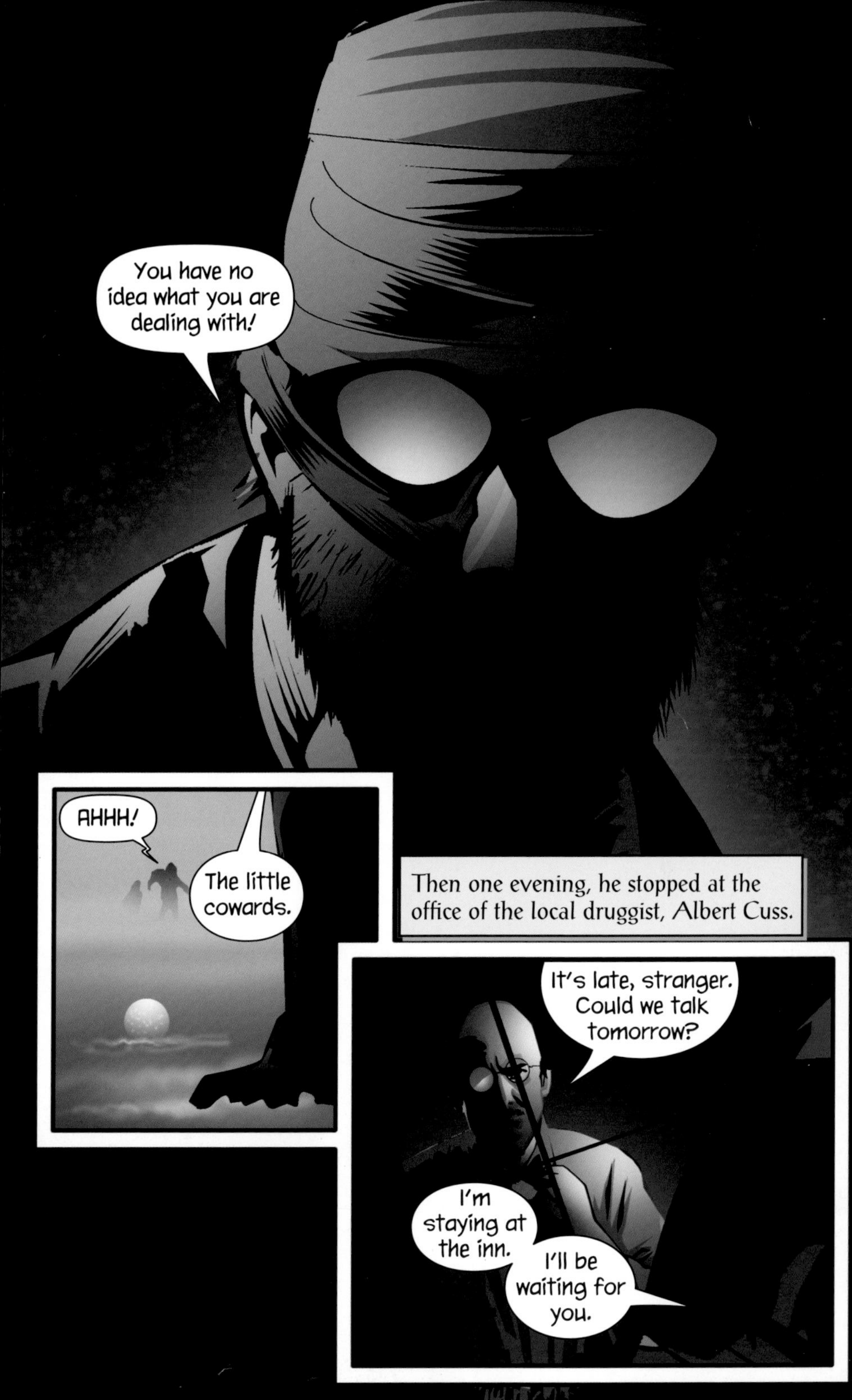
You have no idea what you are dealing with!
AHHH!
The little cowards.
Then one evening, he stopped at the office of the local druggist, Albert Cuss.
It's late, stranger. Could we talk tomorrow?
I'm staying at the inn.
I'll be waiting for you.

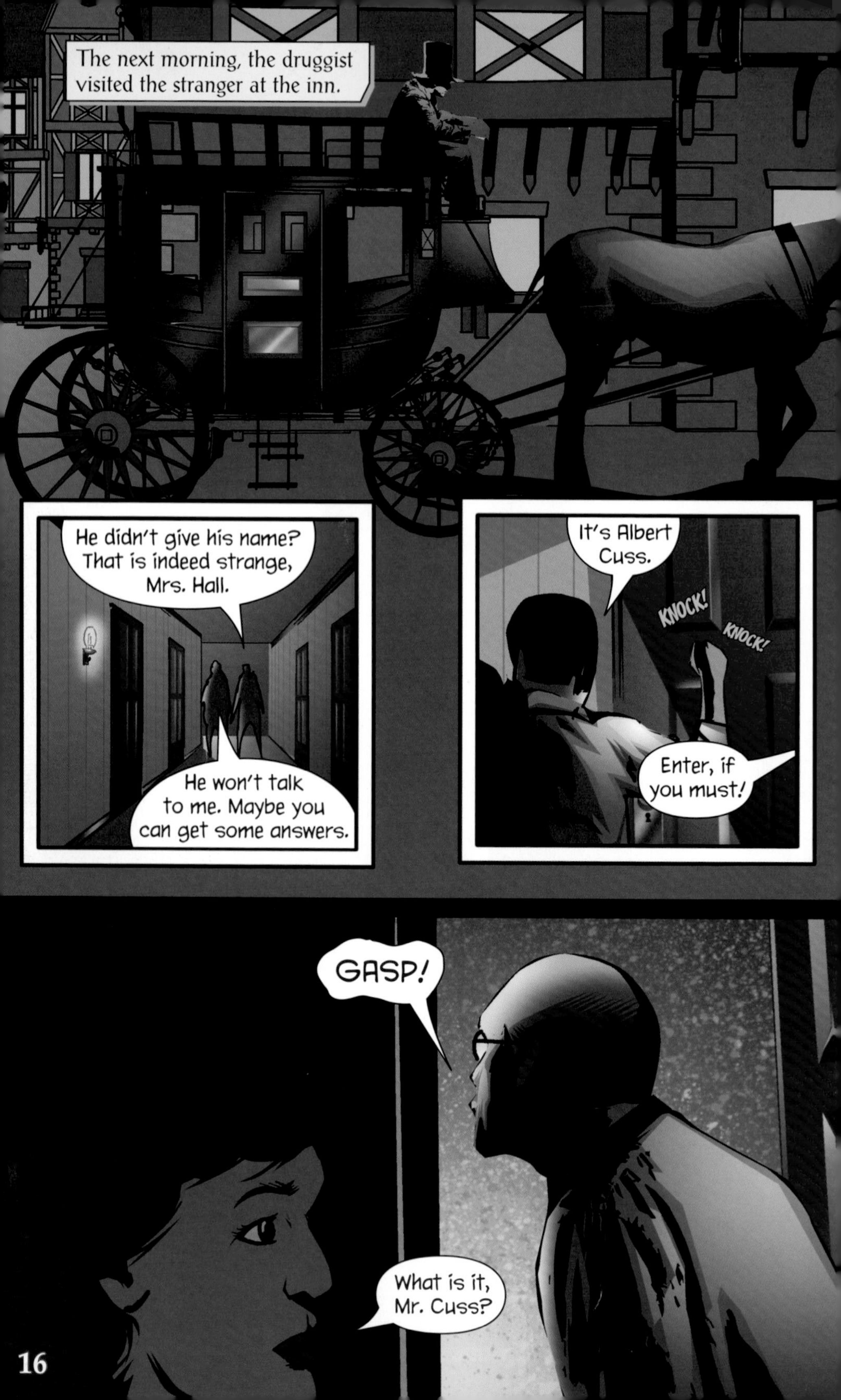
The next morning, the druggist visited the stranger at the inn.
He didn't give his name? That is indeed strange, Mrs. Hall.
He won't talk to me. Maybe you can get some answers.
It's Albert Cuss.
KNOCK! KNOCK!
Enter, if you must!
GASP!
What is it, Mr. Cuss?

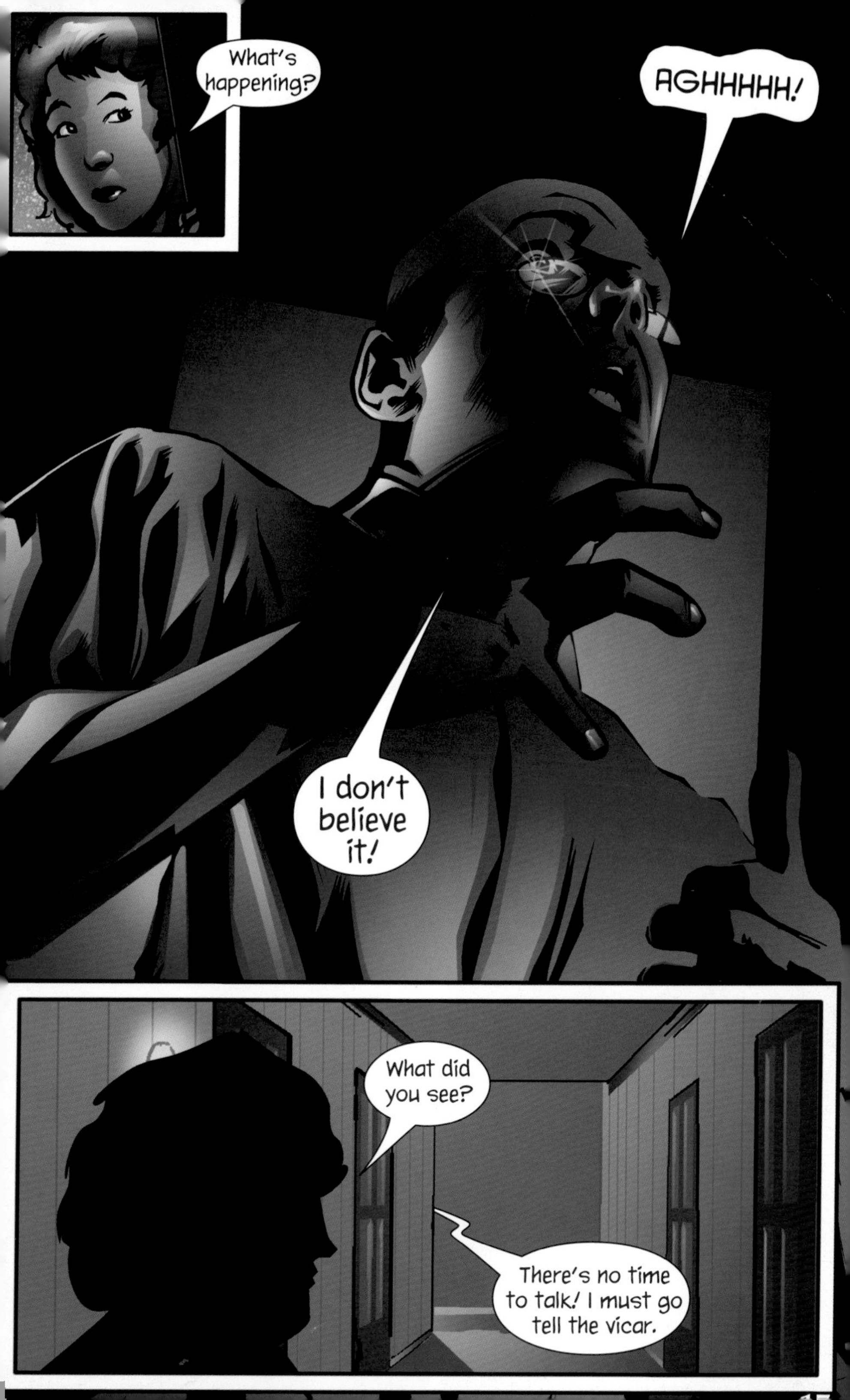
What's happening?
AGHHHHH!
I don't believe it!
What did you see?
There's no time to talk! I must go tell the vicar.

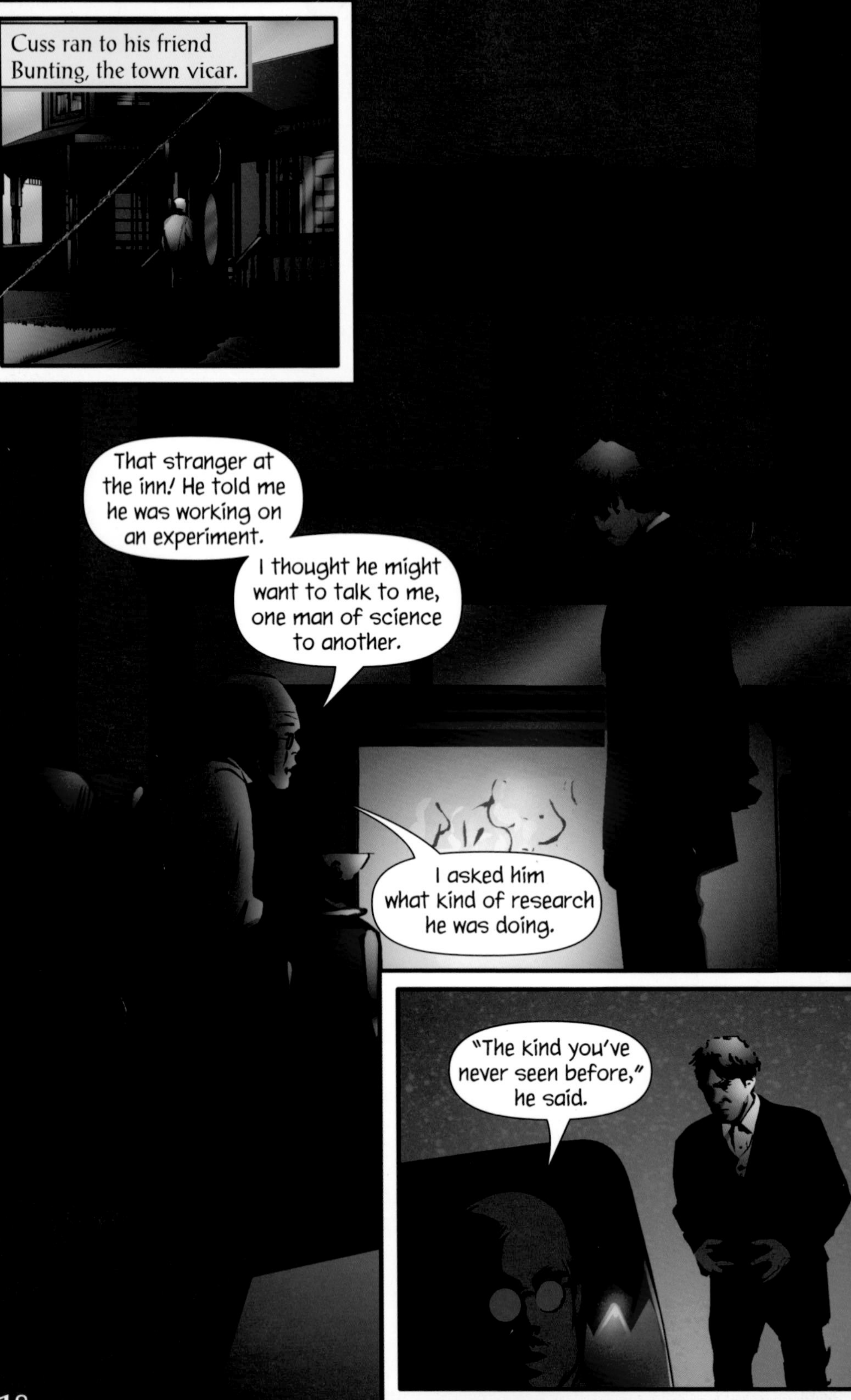
Cuss ran to his friend Bunting, the town vicar.
That stranger at the inn! He told me he was working on an experiment.
I thought he might want to talk to me, one man of science to another.
I asked him what kind of research he was doing.
"The kind you've never seen before," he said.

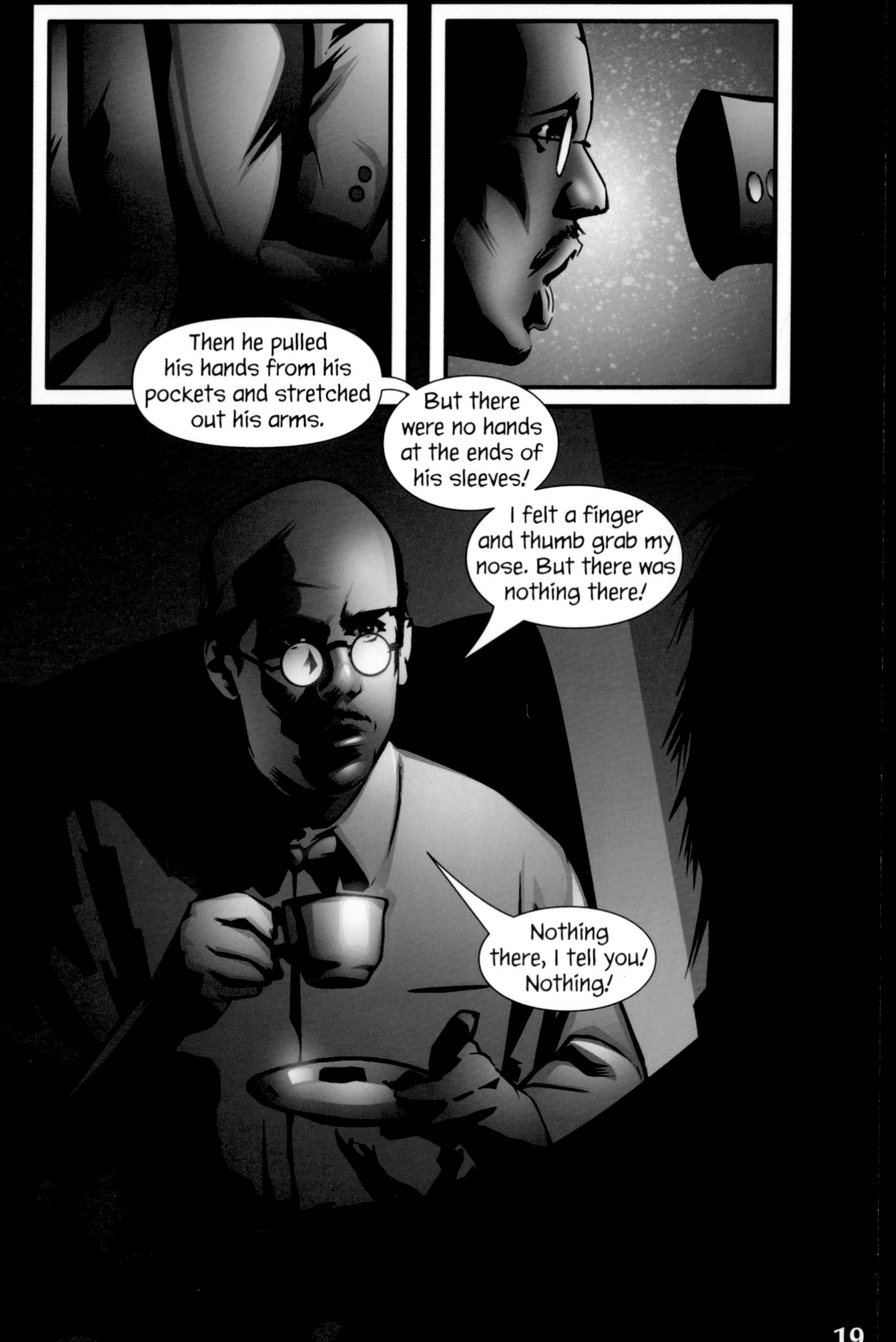
Then he pulled his hands from his pockets and stretched out his arms.
But there were no hands at the ends of his sleeves!
I felt a finger and thumb grab my nose. But there was nothing there!
Nothing there, I tell you! Nothing!

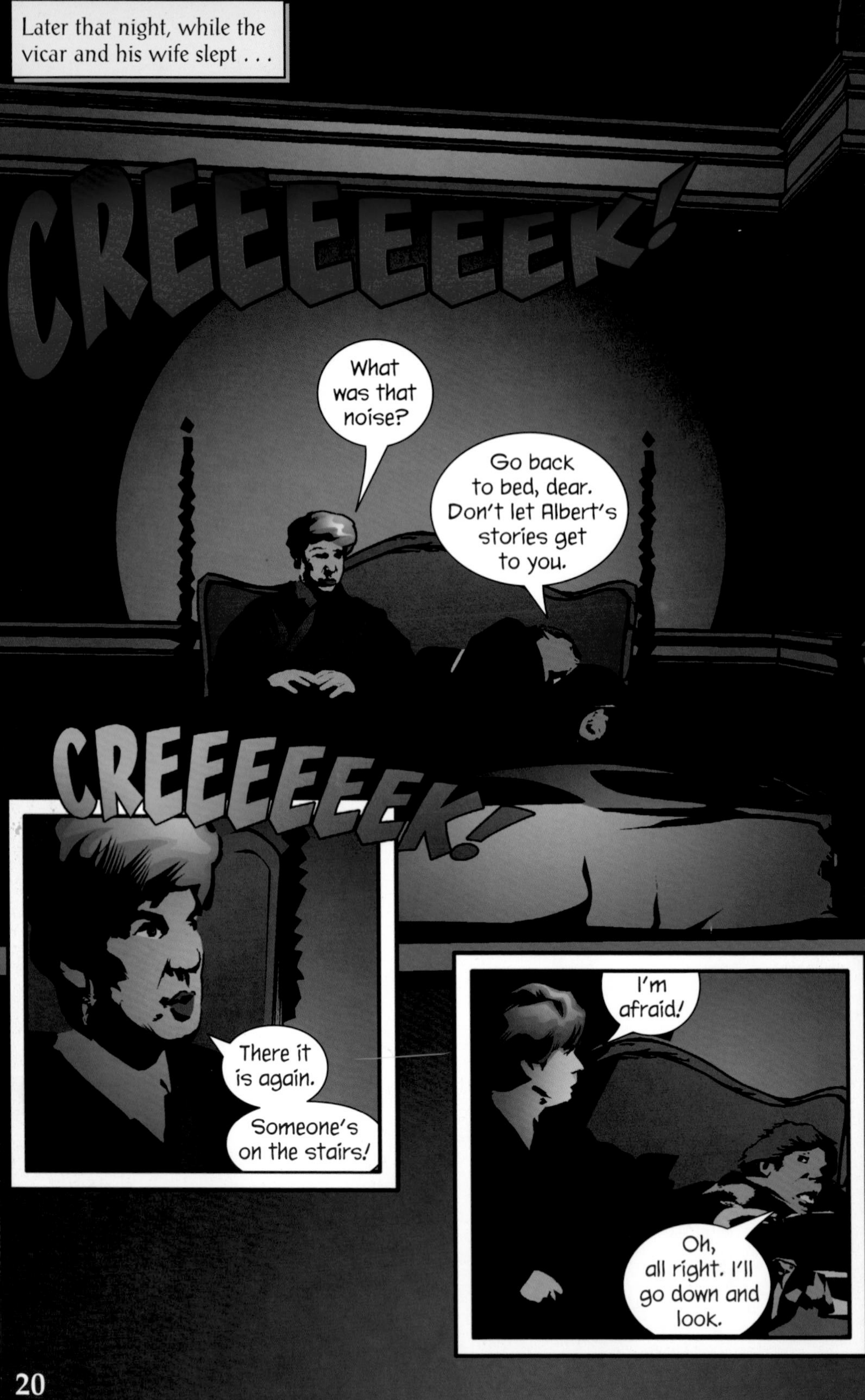
Later that night, while the vicar and his wife slept . . .
CREEEEEEK!
What was that noise?
Go back to bed, dear. Don't let Albert's stories get to you.
CREEEEEEK!
There it is again.
Someone's on the stairs!
I'm afraid!
Oh, all right. I'll go down and look.

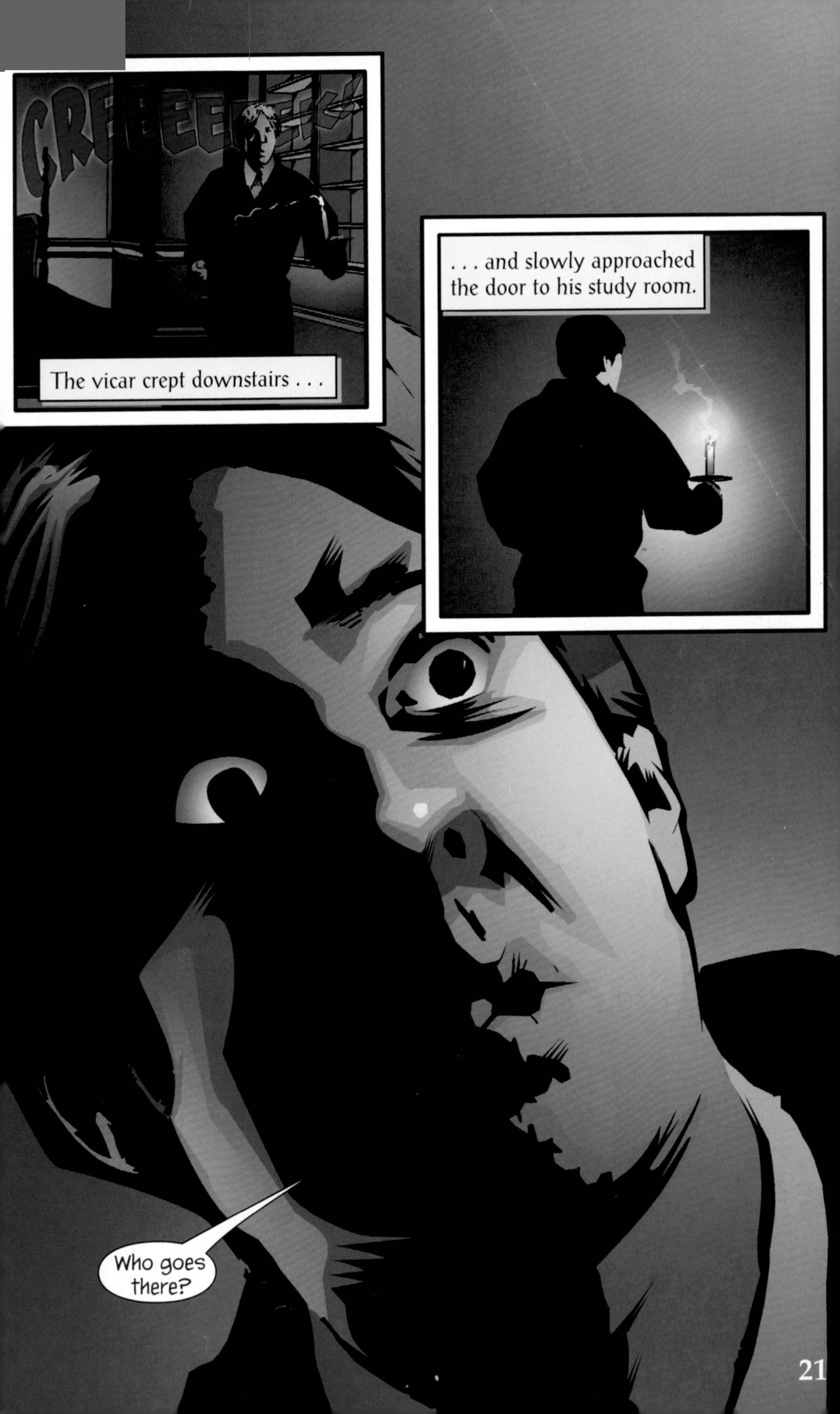
The vicar crept downstairs . . .
. . . and slowly approached the door to his study room.
Who goes there?

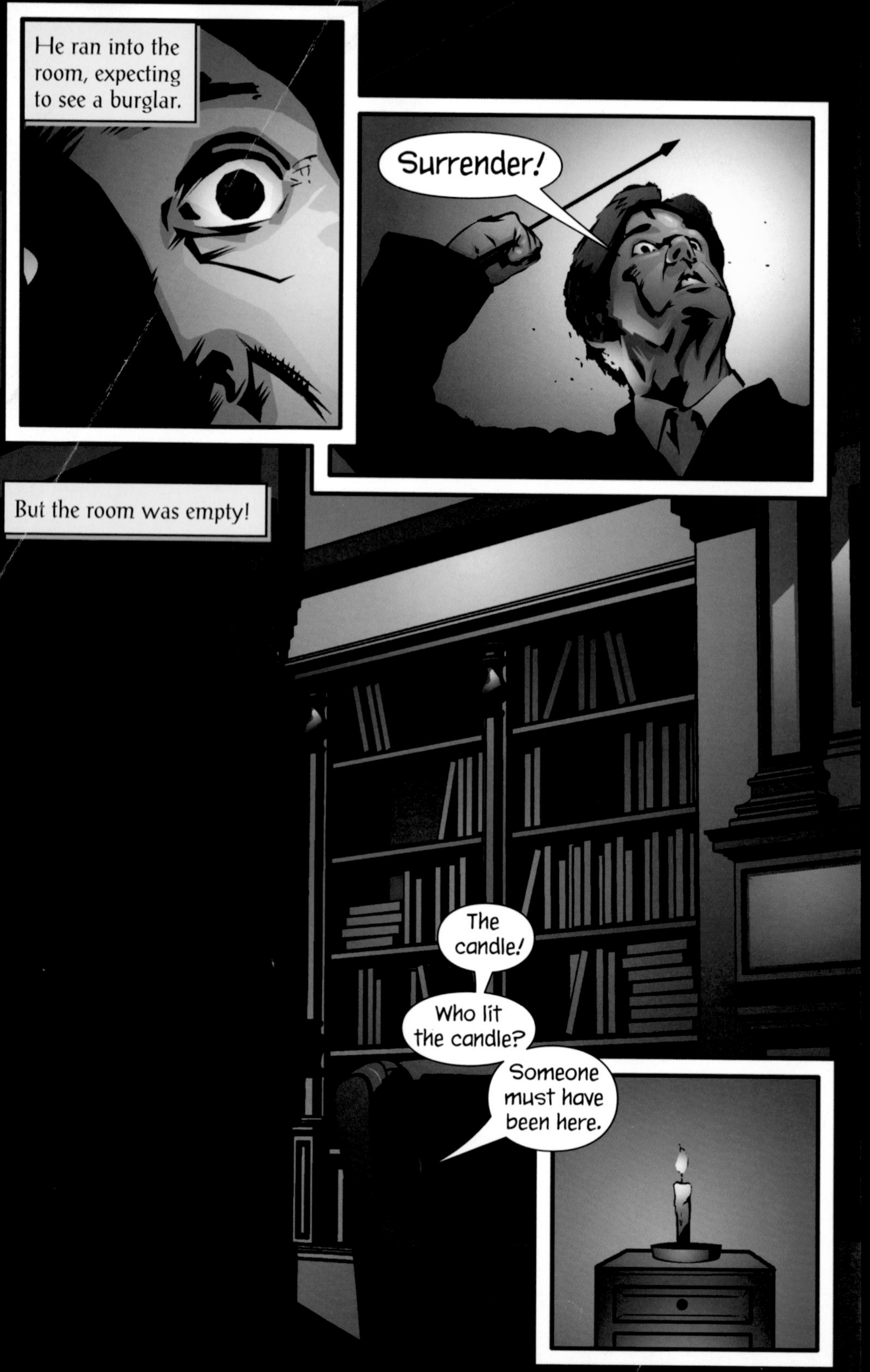
He ran into the room, expecting to see a burglar.
Surrender!
But the room was empty!
The candle!
Who lit the candle?
Someone must have been here.

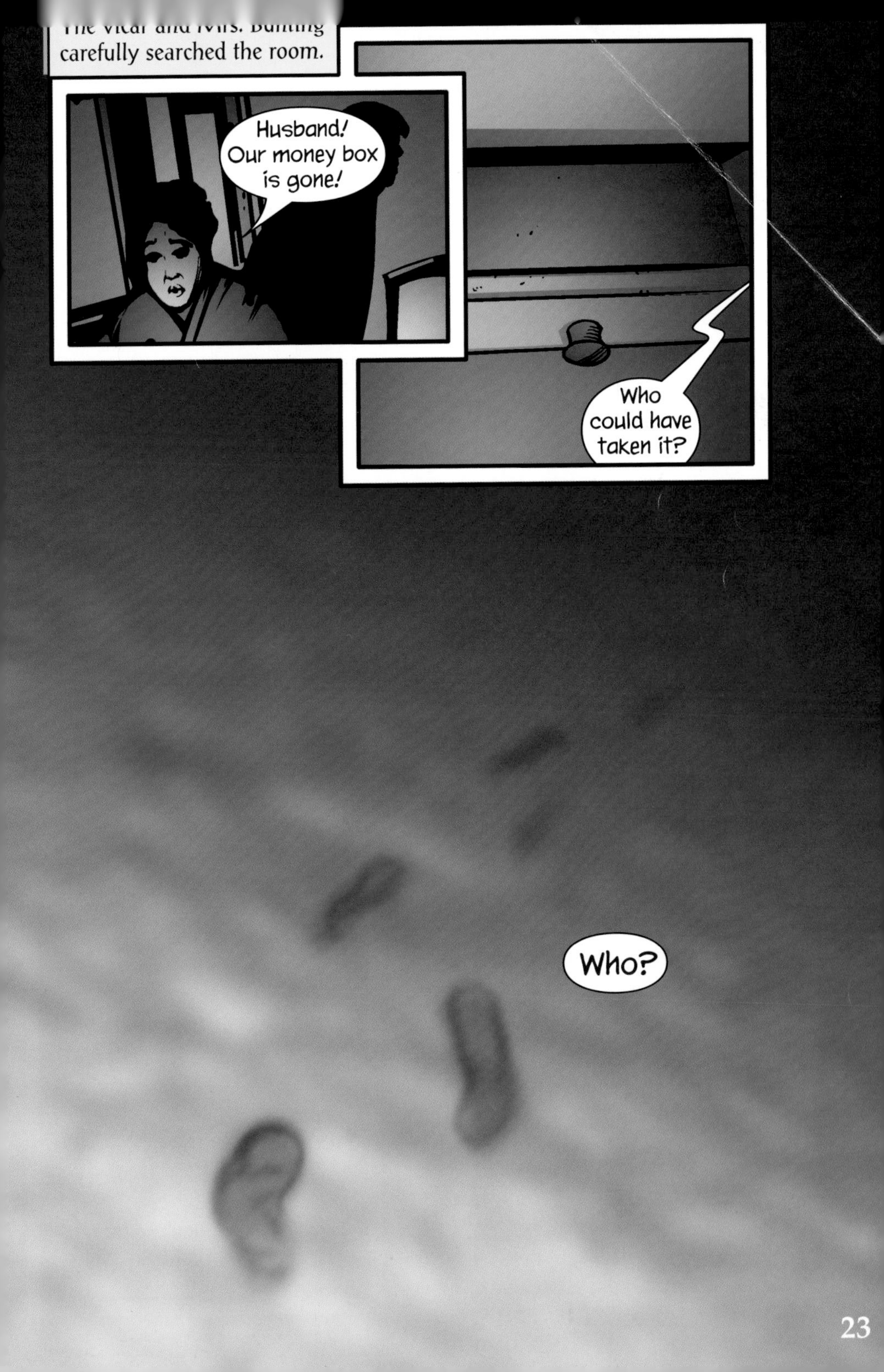
carefully searched the room.
Husband! Our money box is gone!
Who could have taken it?
Who?

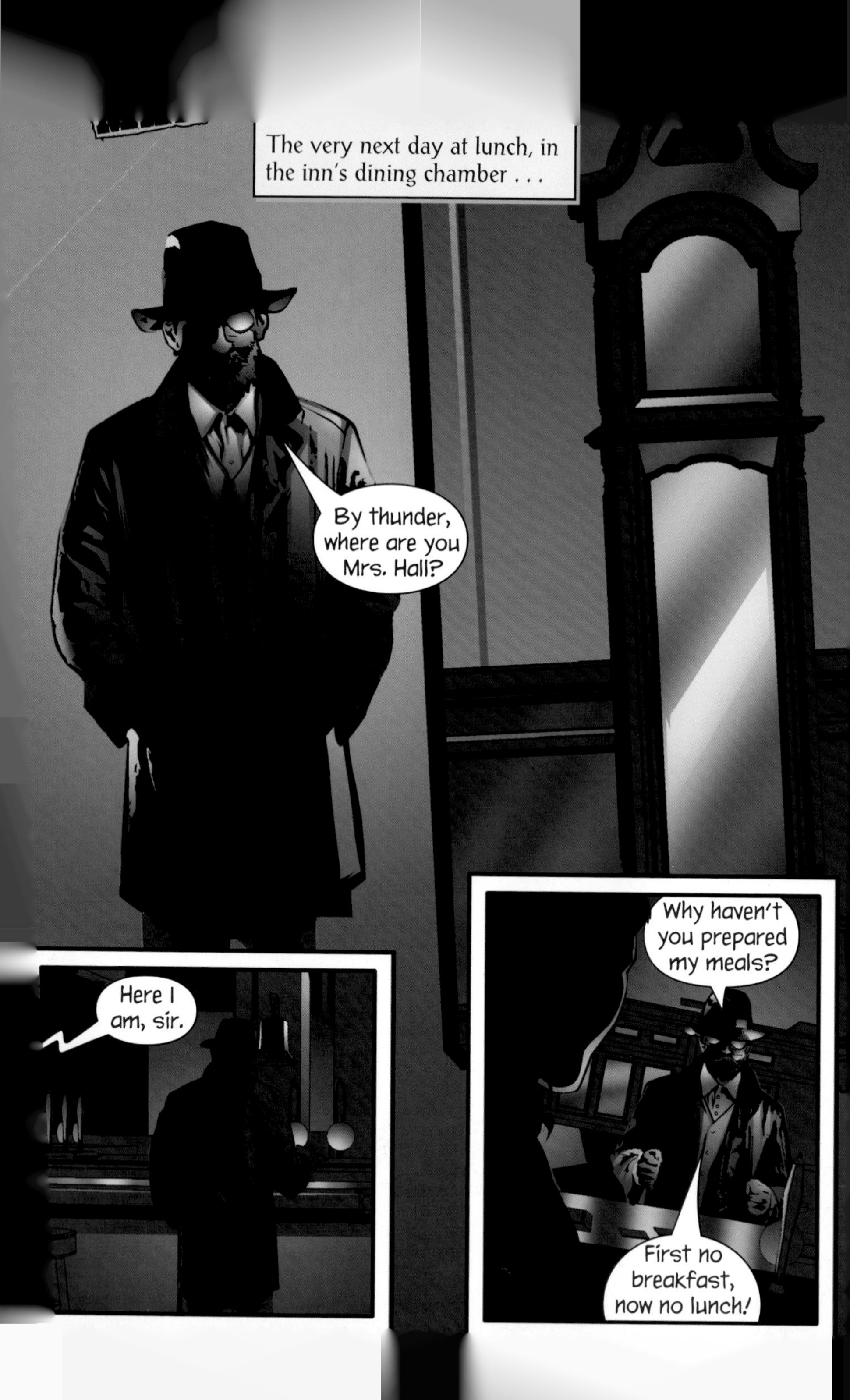

The very next day at lunch, in the inn's dining chamber . . .
By thunder, where are you Mrs. Hall?
Here I am, sir.
Why haven't you prepared my meals?
First no breakfast, now no lunch!

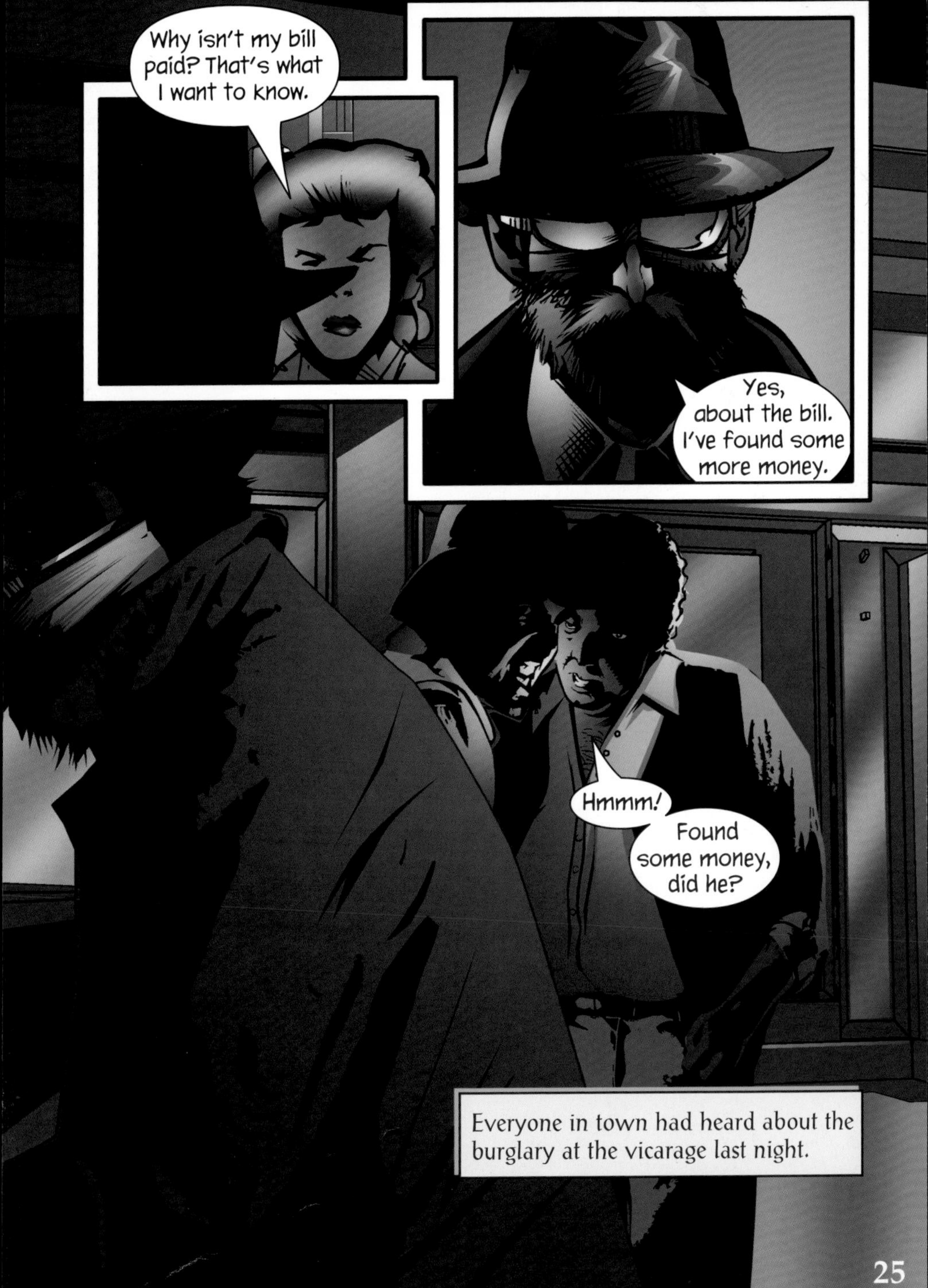
Why isn't my bill paid? That's what I want to know.
Yes, about the bill. I've found some more money.
Hmmm!
Found some money, did he?
Everyone in town had heard about the burglary at the vicarage last night.

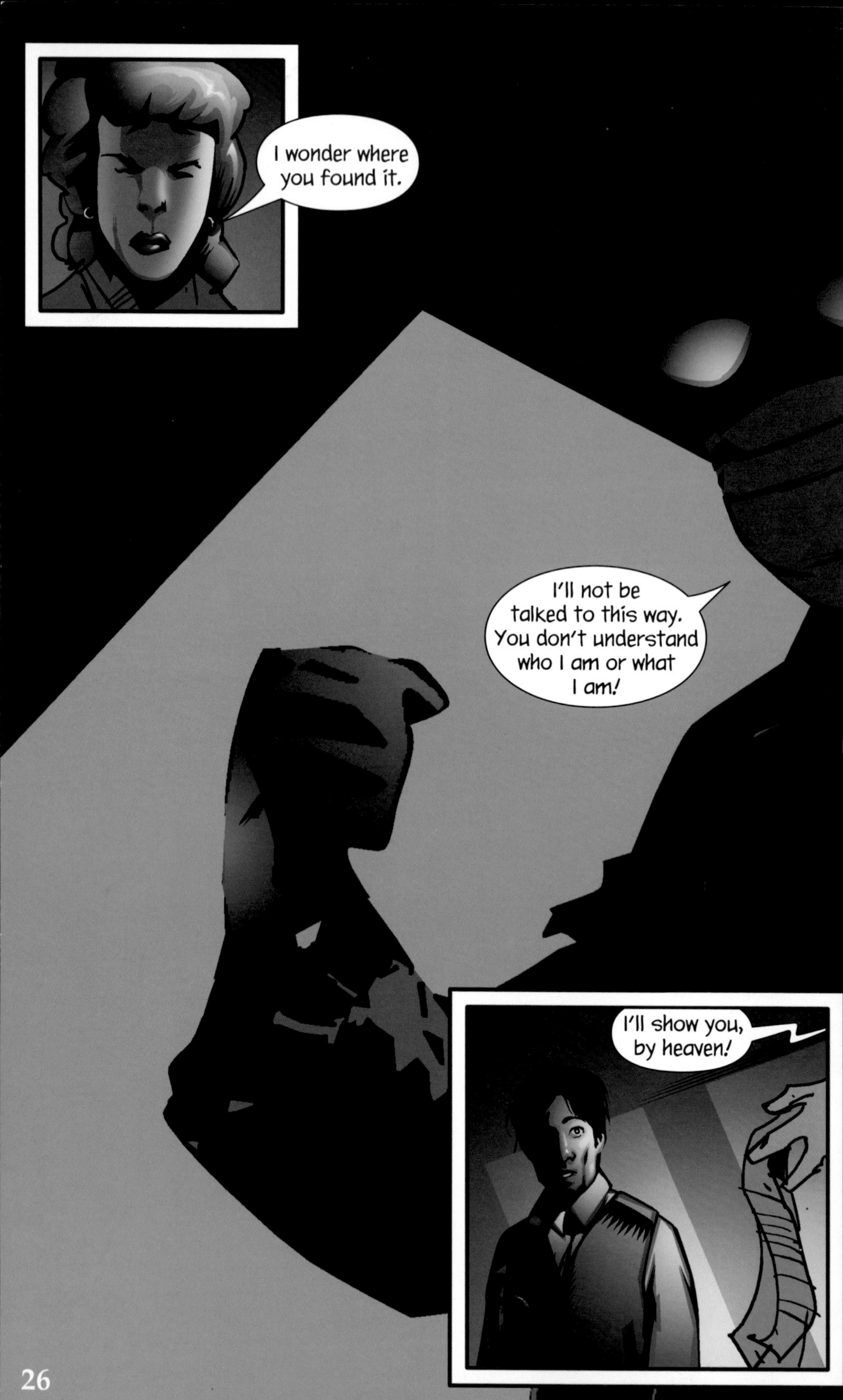
I wonder where you found it.
I'll not be talked to this way. You don't understand who I am or what I am!
I'll show you, by heaven!

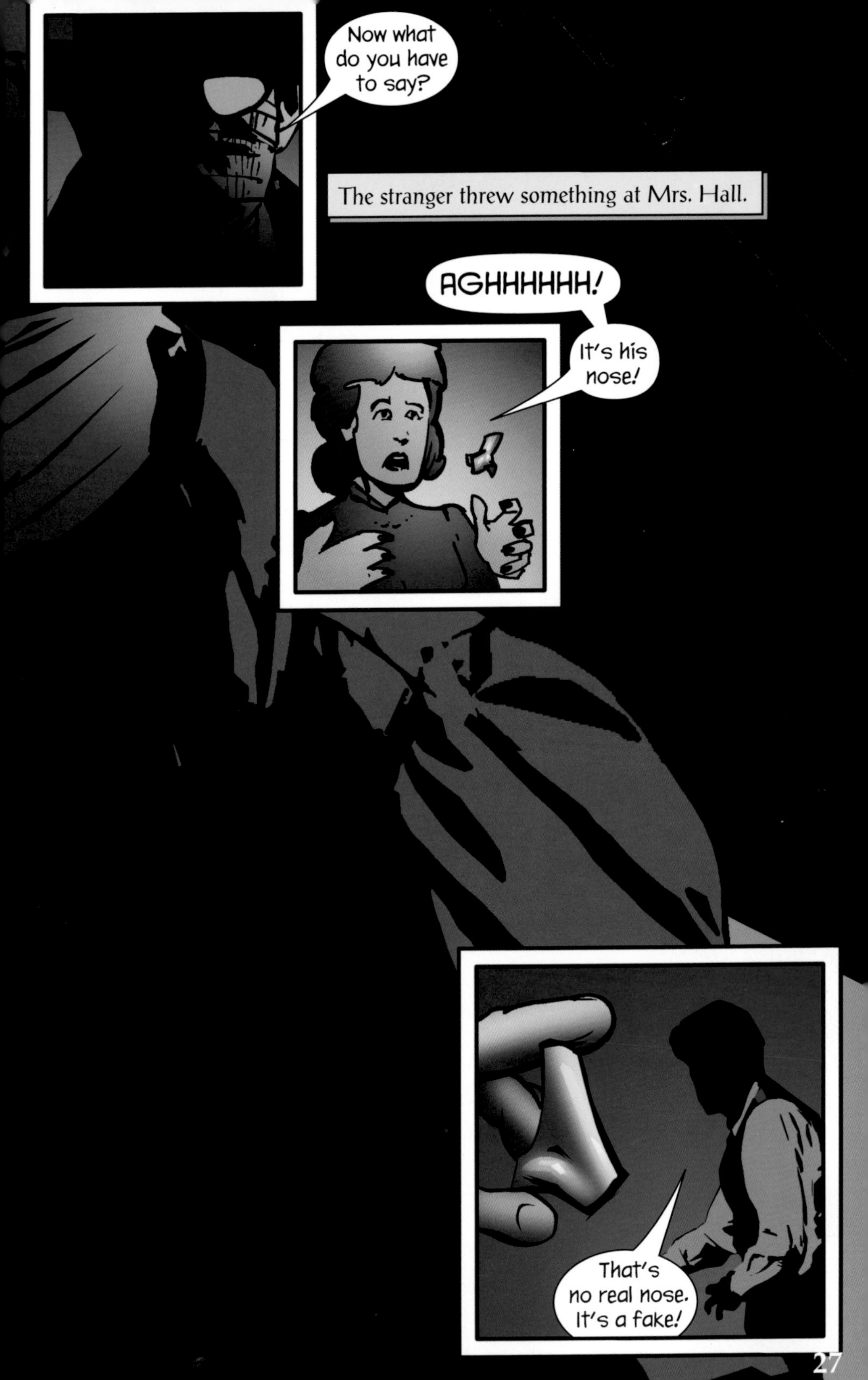
Now what do you have to say?
The stranger threw something at Mrs. Hall.
AGHHHHHH!
It's his nose!
That's no real nose. It's a fake!

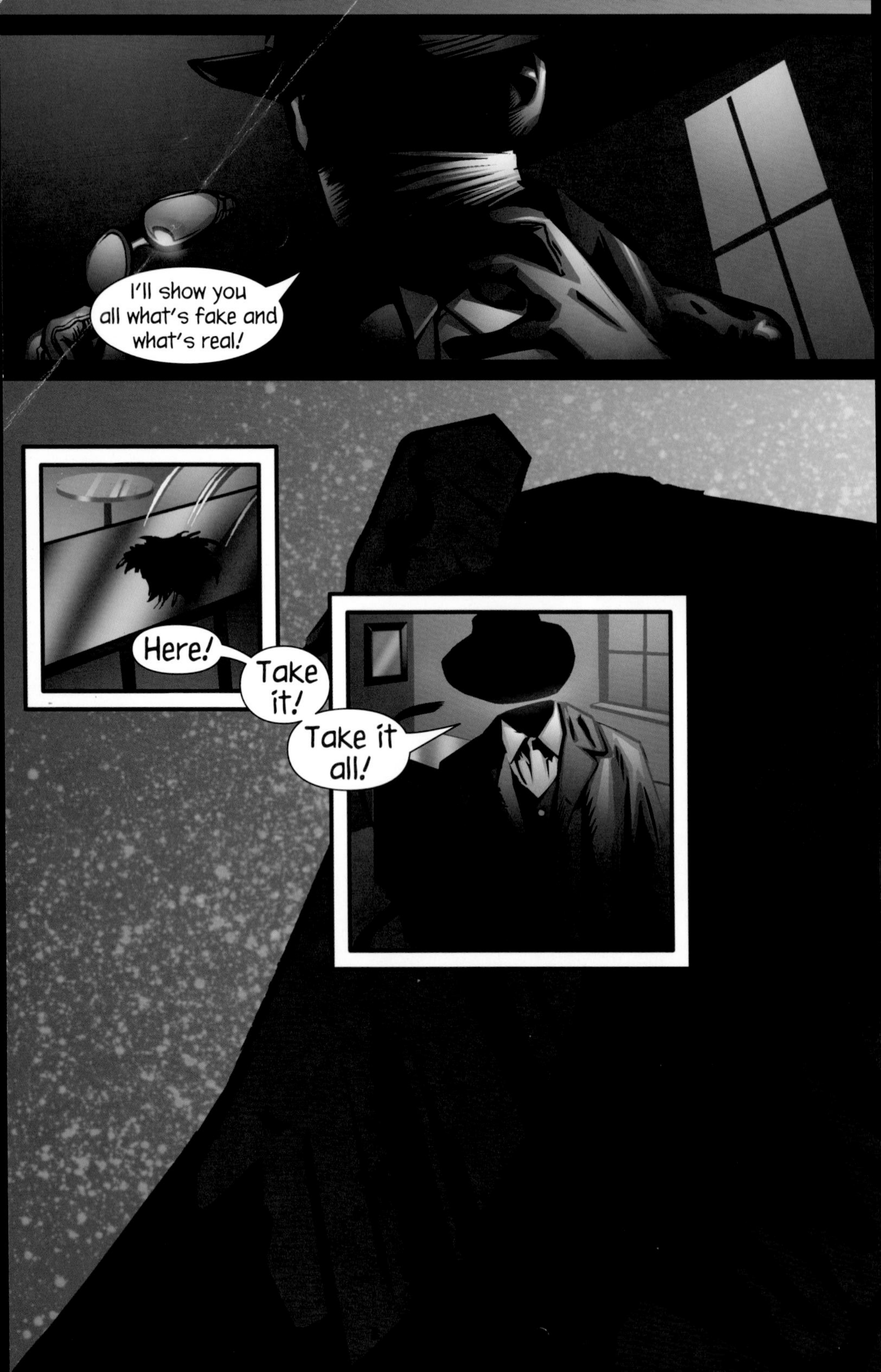
I'll show you all what's fake and what's real!
Here!
Take it!
Take it all!

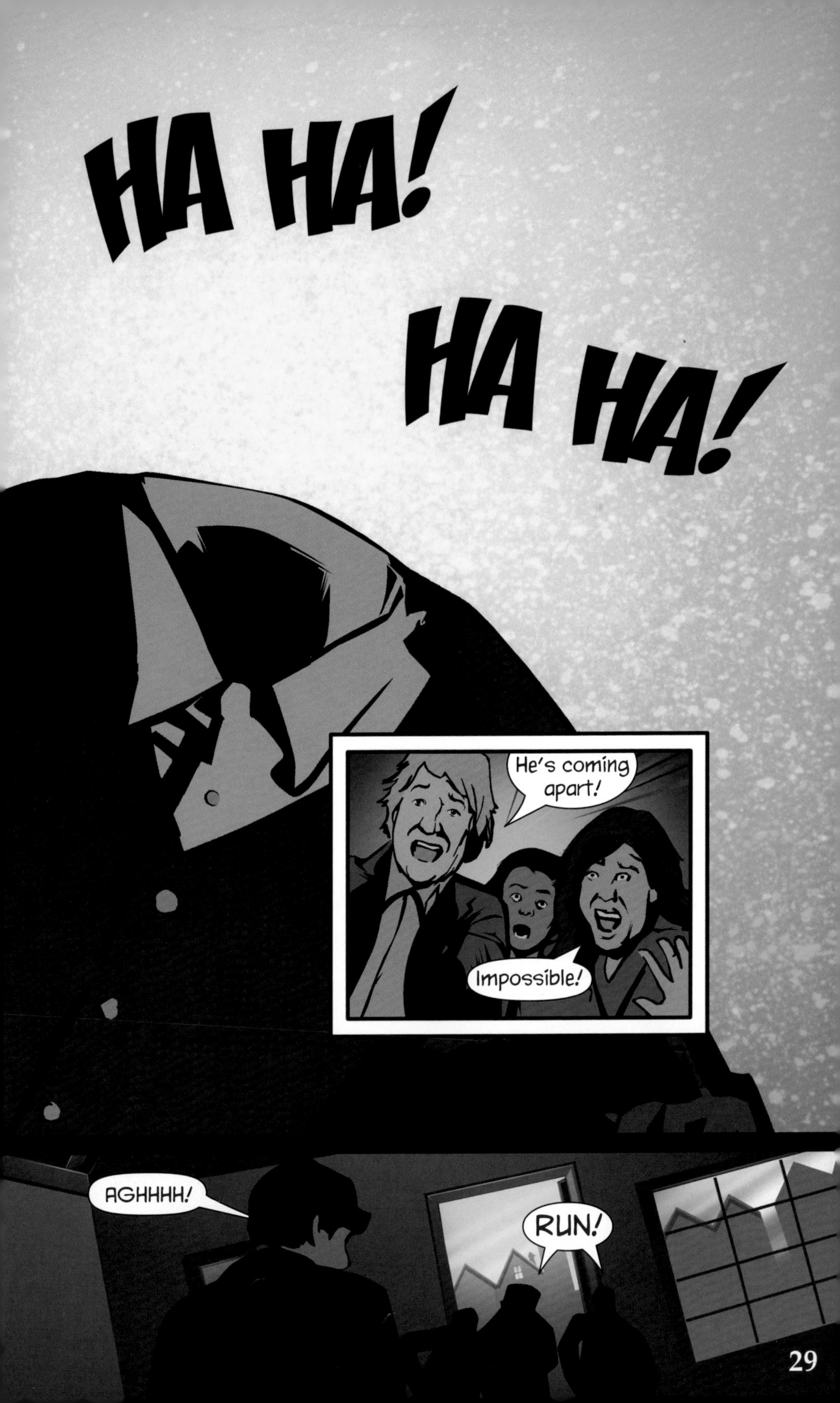
HA HA!
HA HA!
He's coming apart!
Impossible!
AGHHHH!
RUN!

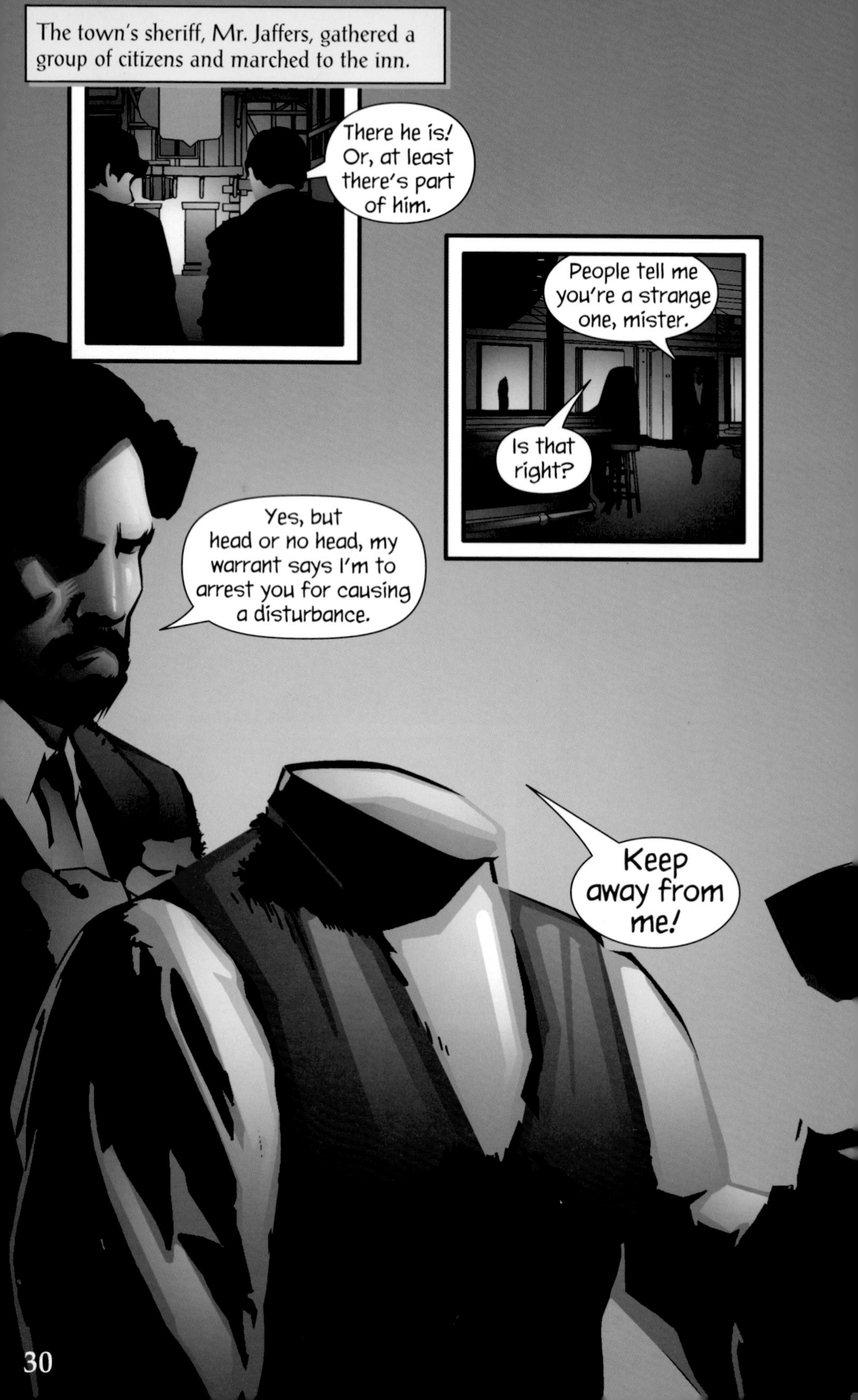

The town's sheriff, Mr. Jaffers, gathered a group of citizens and marched to the inn.
There he is! Or, at least there's part of him.
People tell me you're a strange one, mister.
Is that right?
Yes, but head or no head, my warrant says I'm to arrest you for causing a disturbance.
Keep away from me!

The Invisible Man grabbed for a knife at the bar.

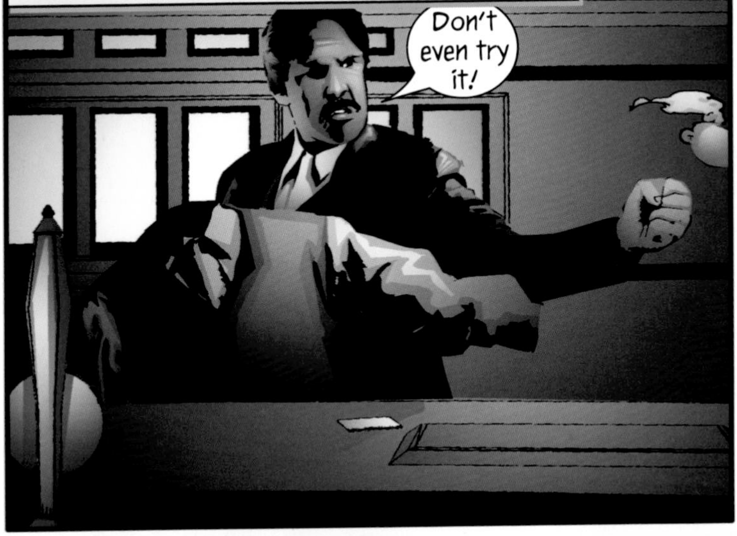
Don't even try it!

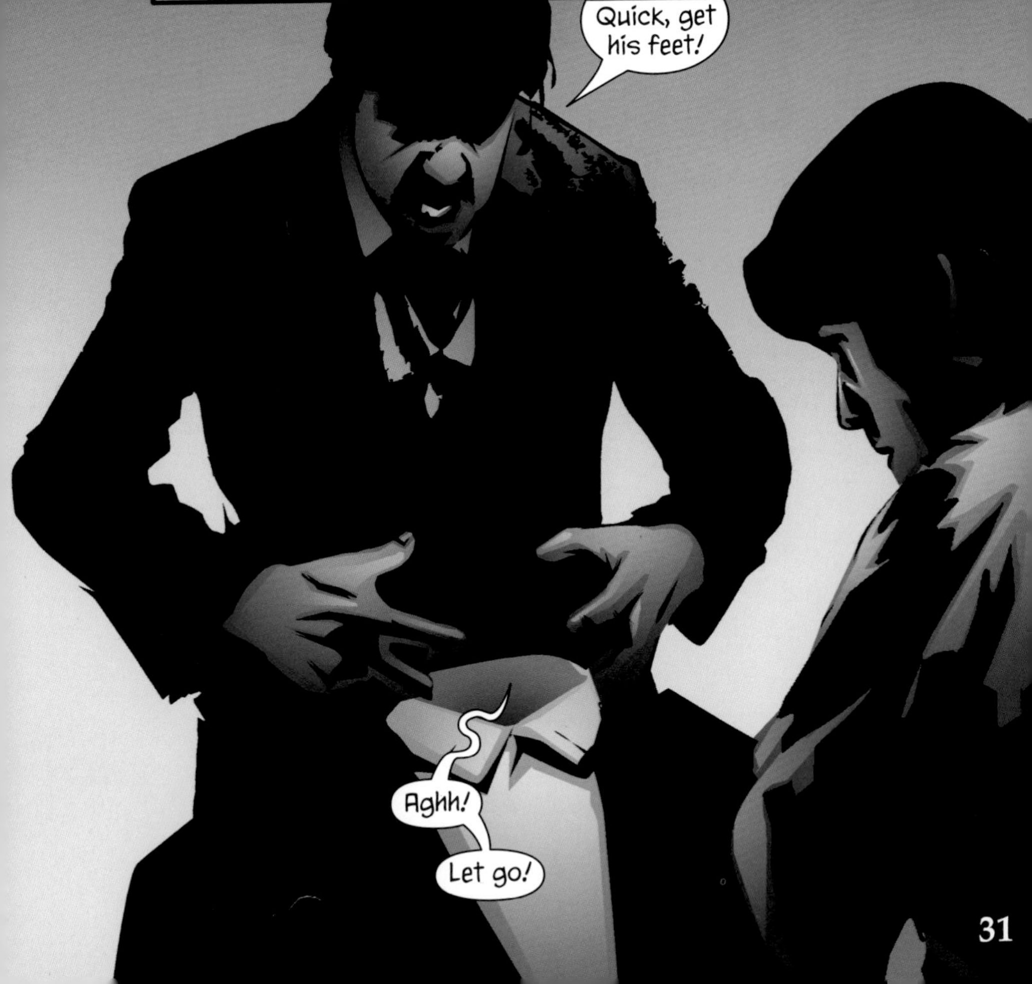
Quick, get his feet!
Aghh!
Let go!

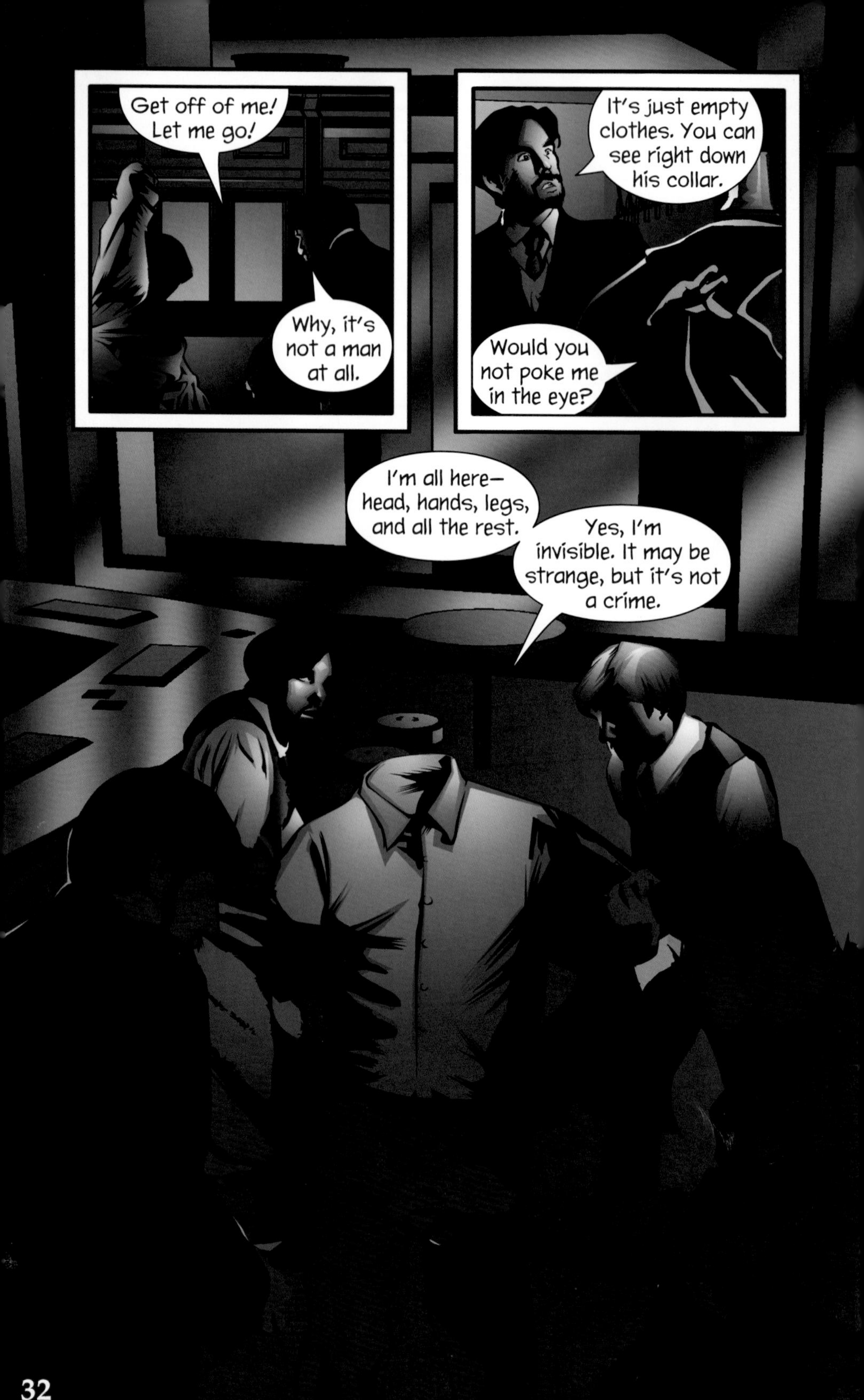
Get off of me! Let me go!
Why, it's not a man at all.
It's just empty clothes. You can see right down his collar.
Would you not poke me in the eye?
I'm all here—head, hands, legs, and all the rest.
Yes, I'm invisible. It may be strange, but it's not a crime.

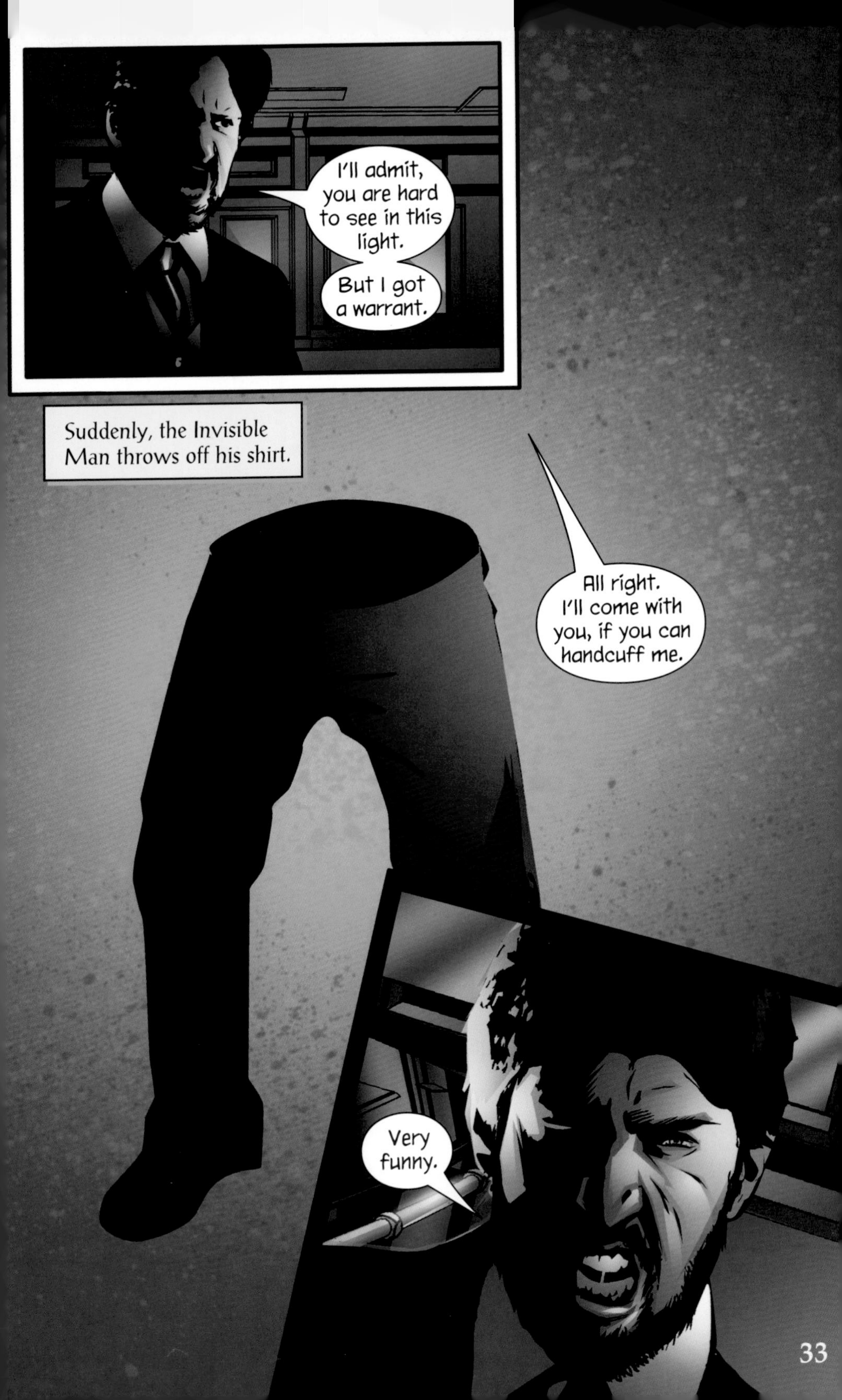
I'll admit, you are hard to see in this light.
But I got a warrant.
Suddenly, the Invisible Man throws off his shirt.
All right. I'll come with you, if you can handcuff me.
Very funny.

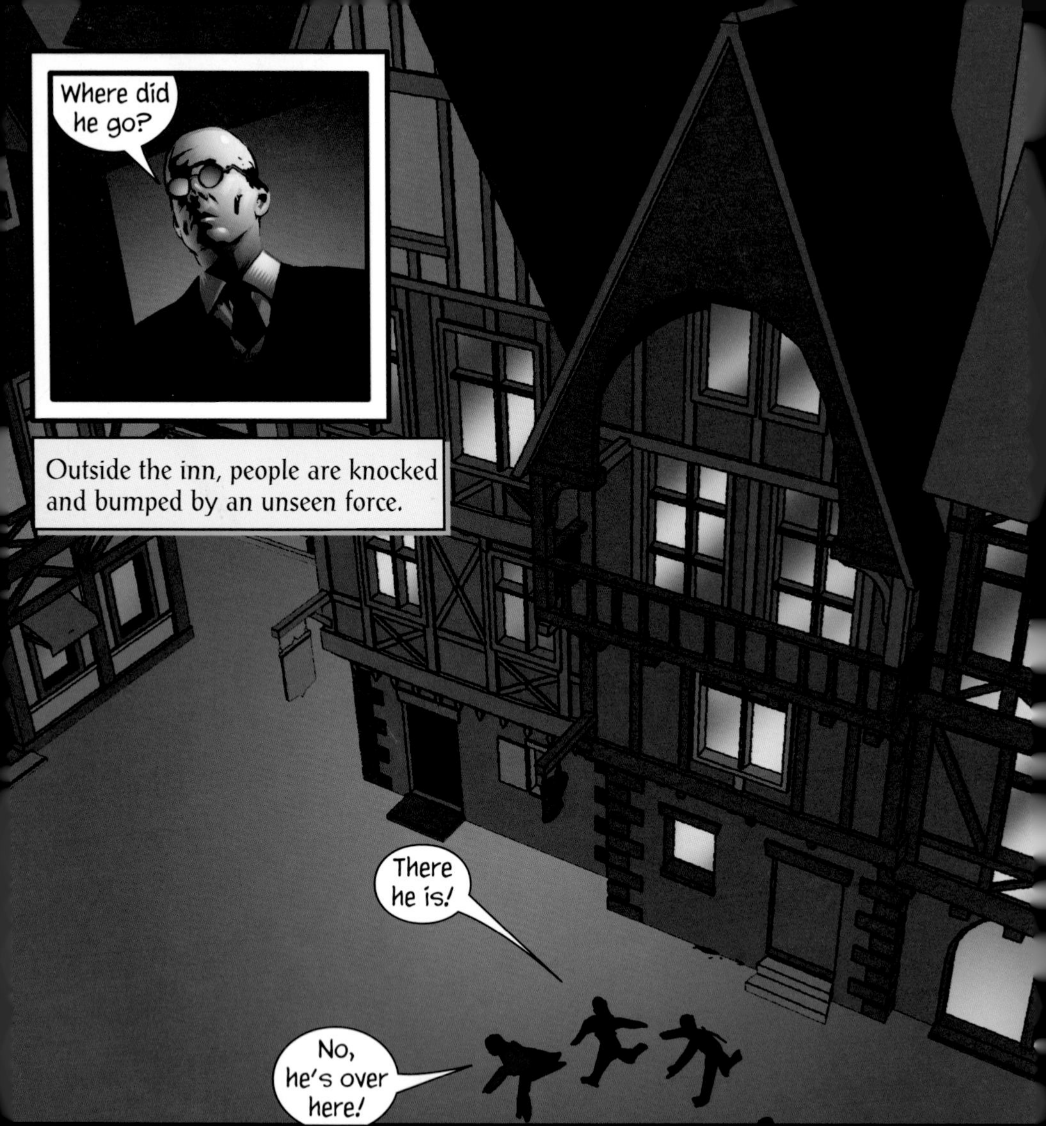
Where did he go?
Outside the inn, people are knocked and bumped by an unseen force.
There he is!
No, he's over here!

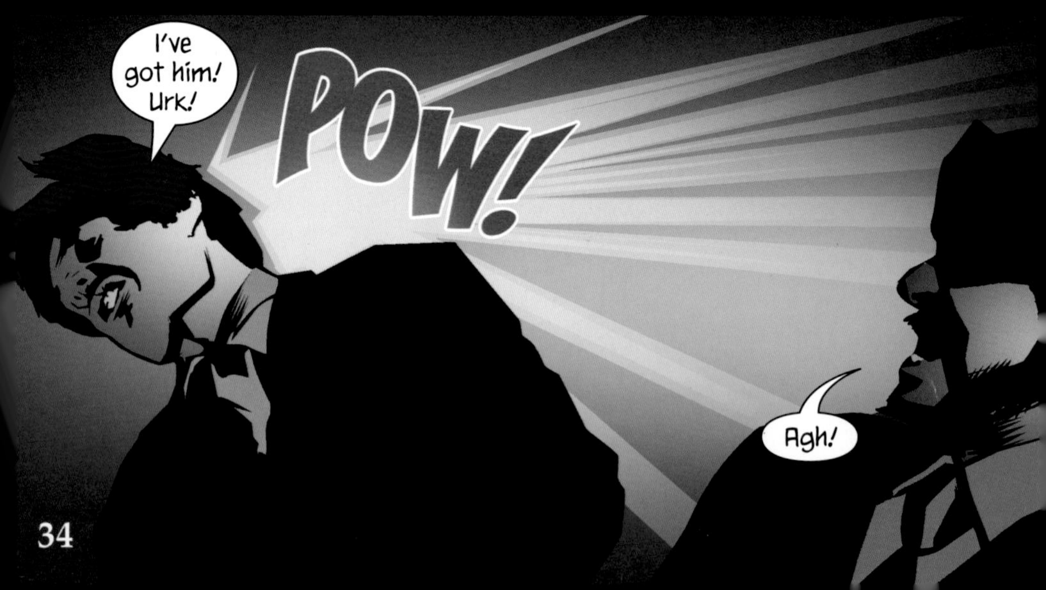
I've got him! Urk!
POW!
Agh!

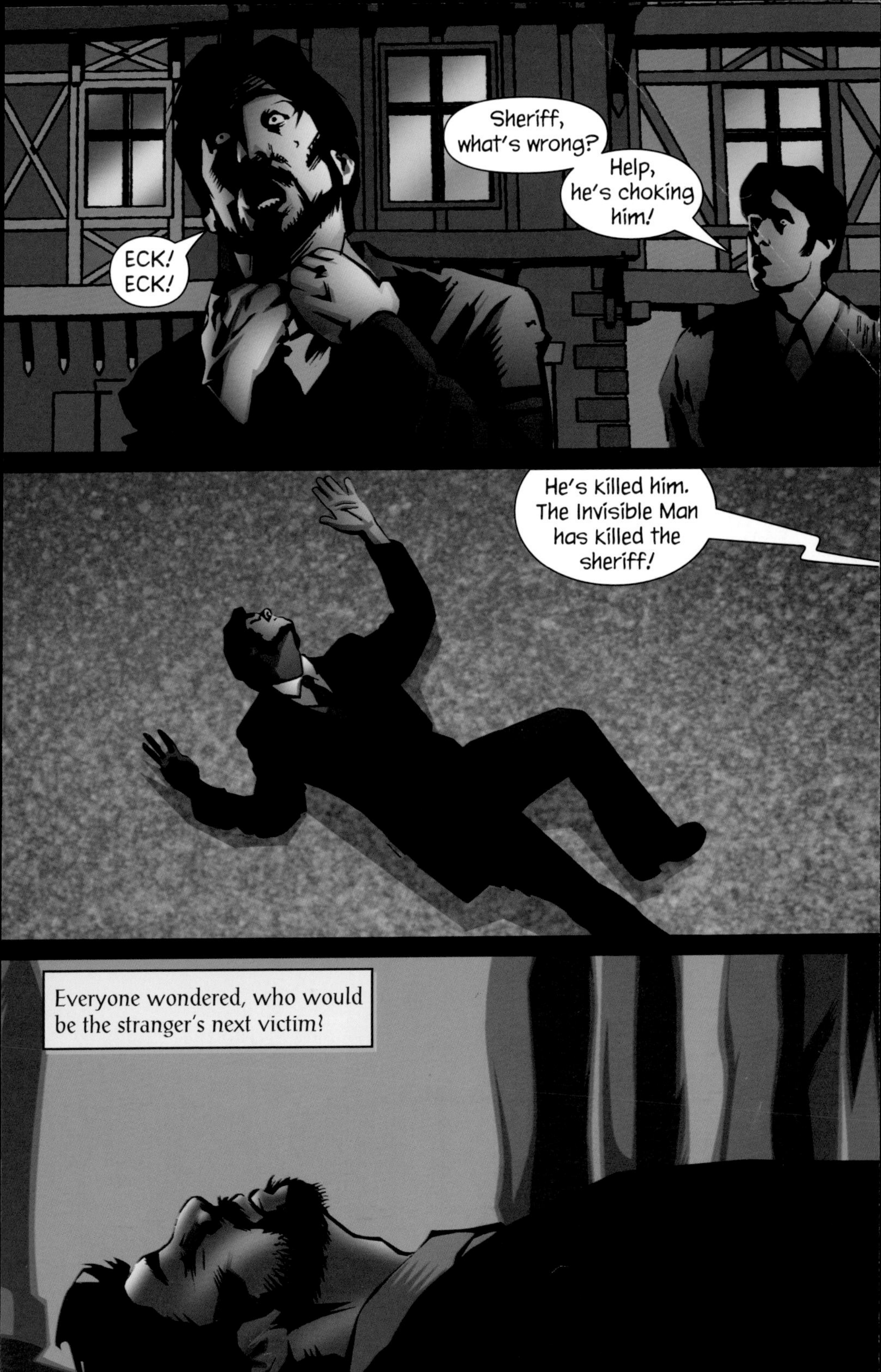
Sheriff, what's wrong?
Help, he's choking him!
ECK! ECK!
He's killed him. The Invisible Man has killed the sheriff!
Everyone wondered, who would be the stranger's next victim?

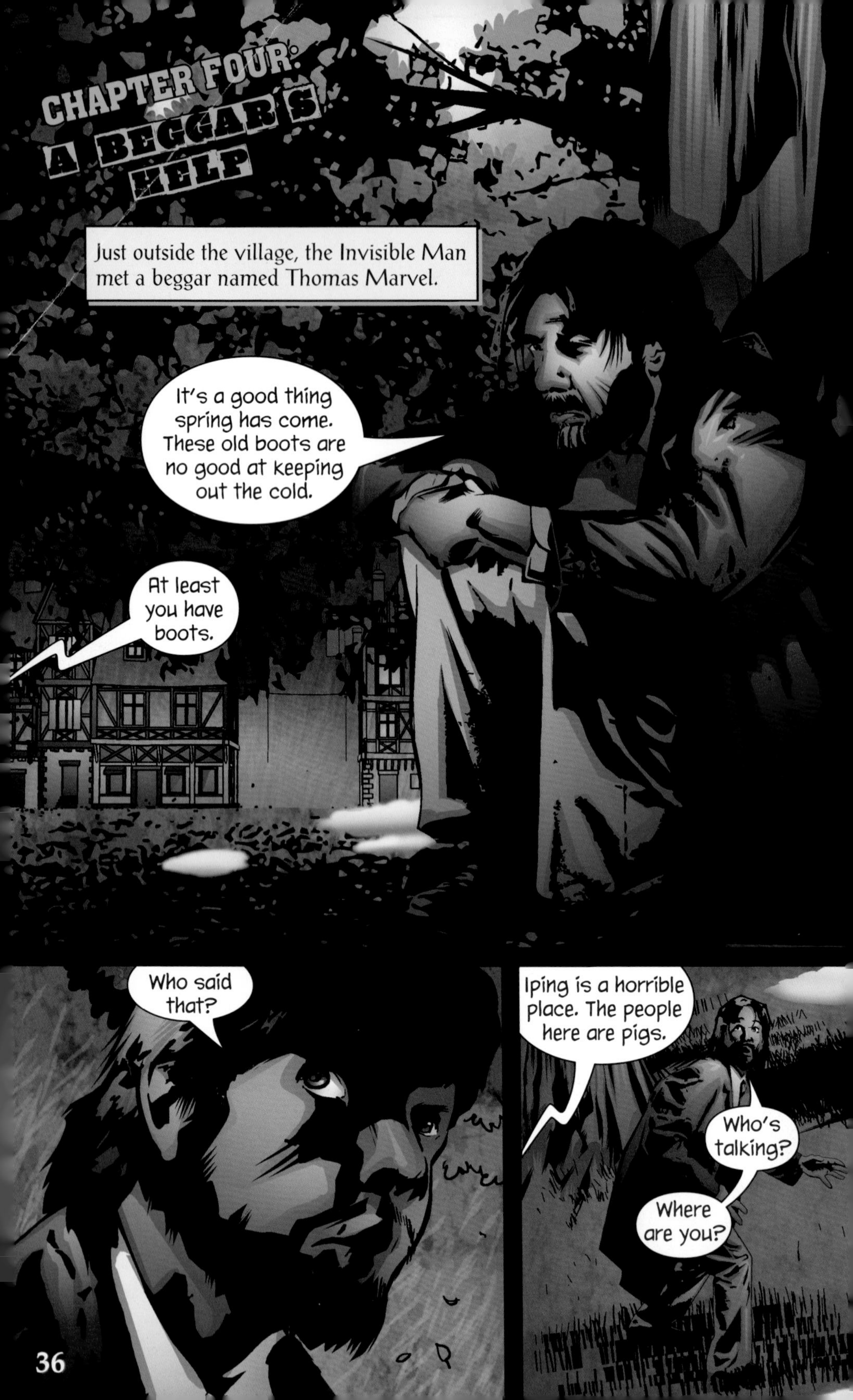
CHAPTER FOUR:
A BEGGAR'S HELP
Just outside the village, the Invisible Man met a beggar named Thomas Marvel.
It's a good thing spring has come. These old boots are no good at keeping out the cold.
At least you have boots.
Who said that?
Iping is a horrible place. The people here are pigs.
Who's talking?
Where are you?

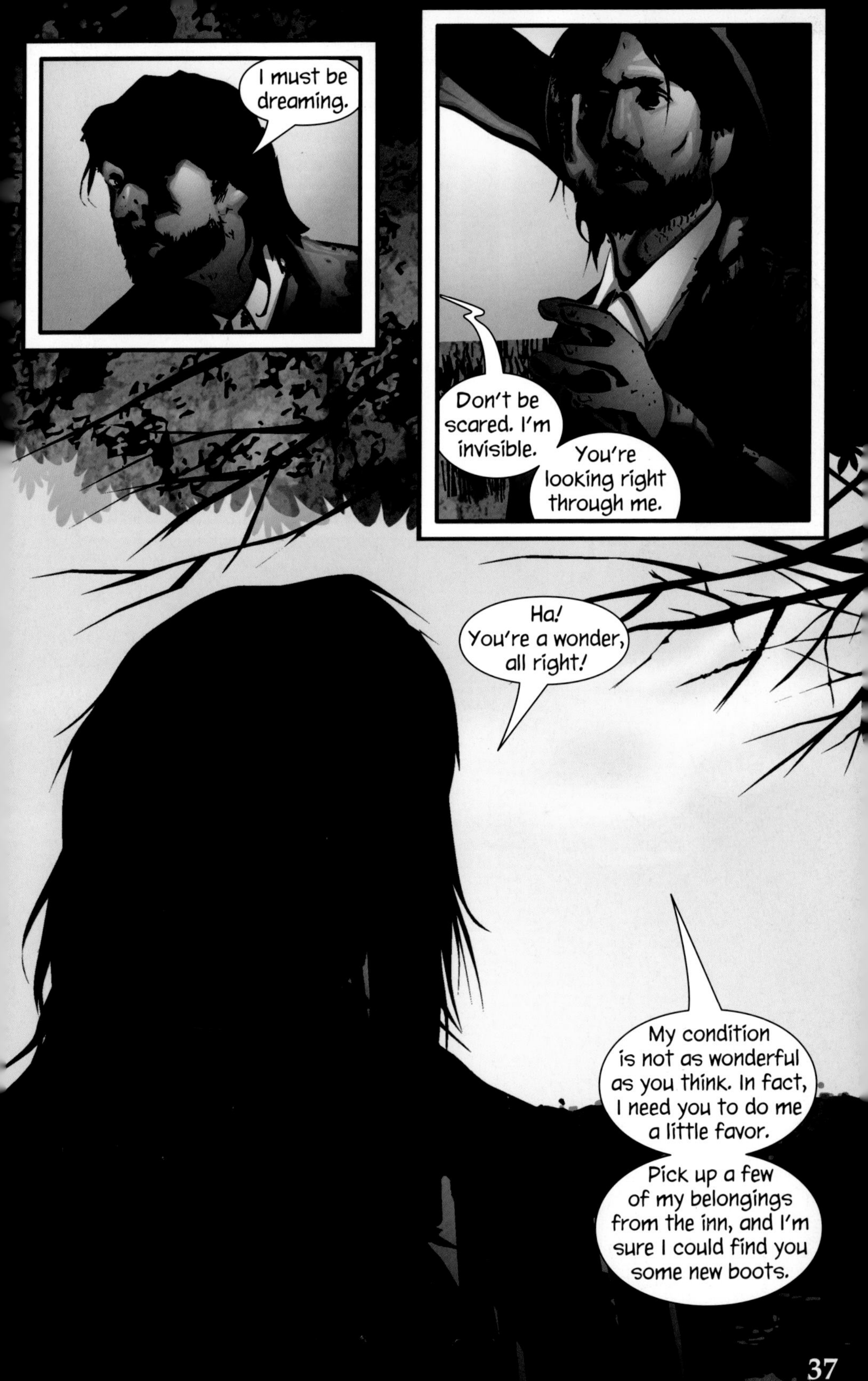
I must be dreaming.
Don't be scared. I'm invisible.
You're looking right through me.
Ha! You're a wonder, all right!
My condition is not as wonderful as you think. In fact, I need you to do me a little favor.
Pick up a few of my belongings from the inn, and I'm sure I could find you some new boots.

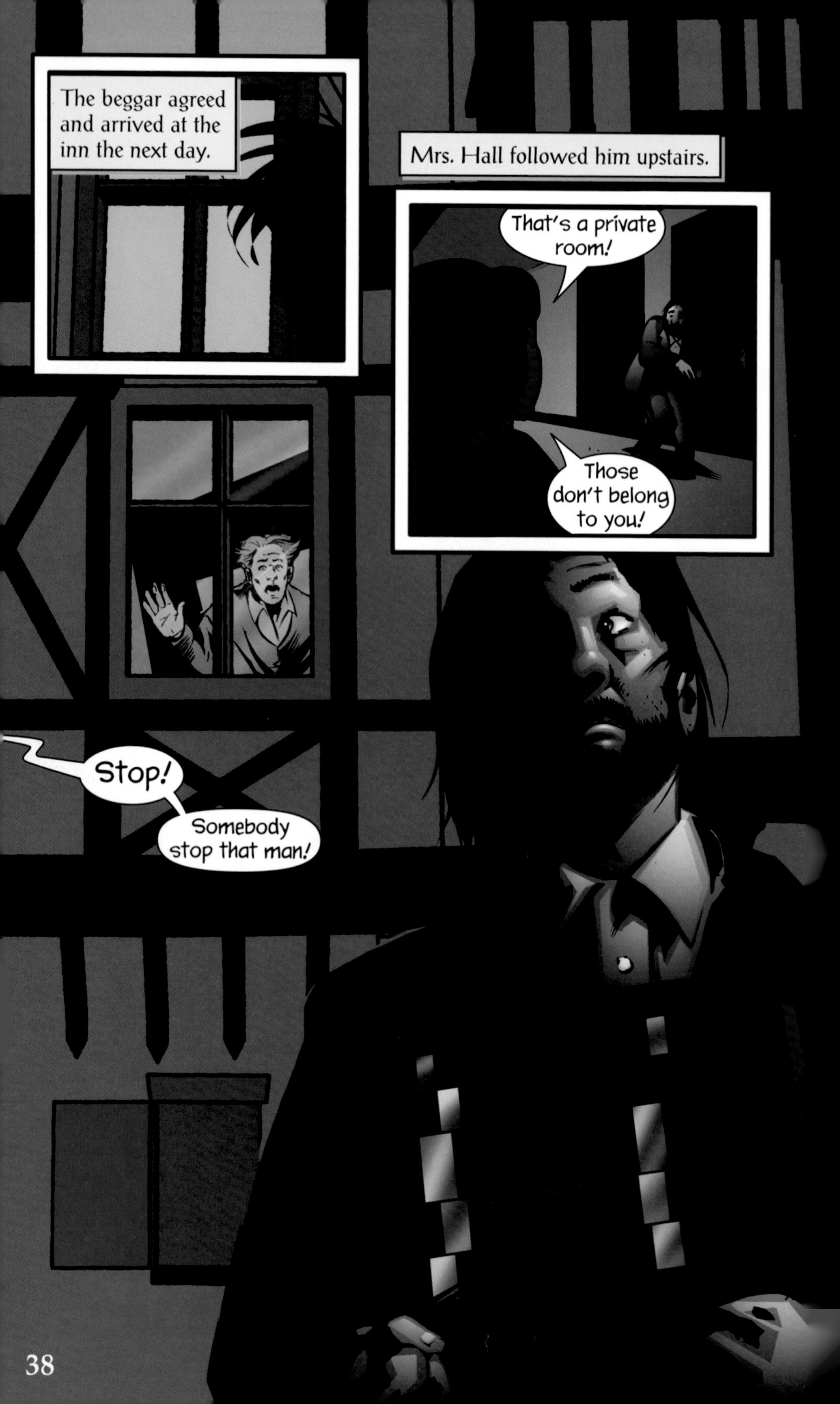

The beggar agreed and arrived at the inn the next day.
Mrs. Hall followed him upstairs.
That's a private room!
Those don't belong to you!
Stop!
Somebody stop that man!

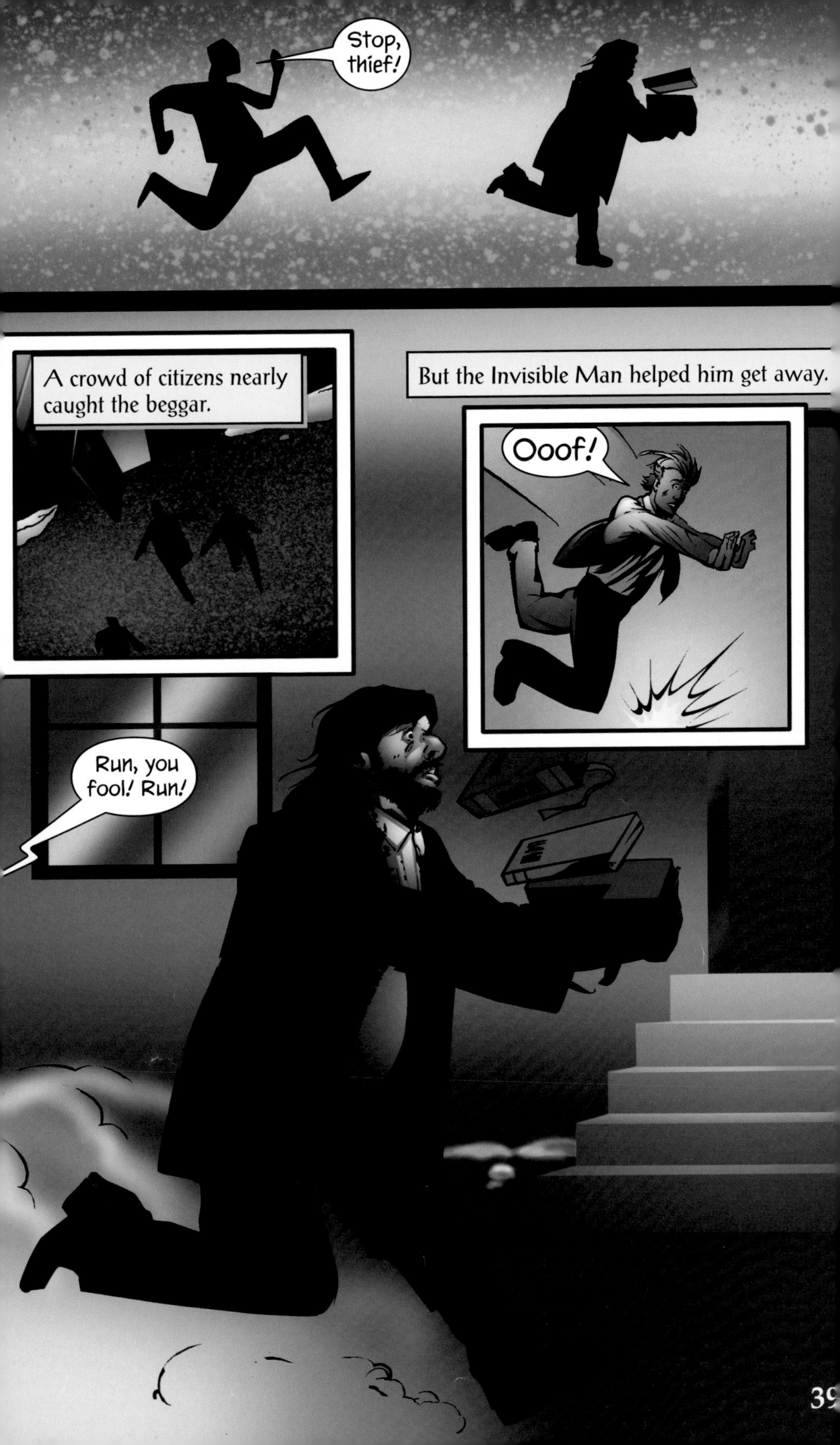

Stop, thief!
A crowd of citizens nearly caught the beggar.
But the Invisible Man helped him get away.
Ooof!
Run, you fool! Run!

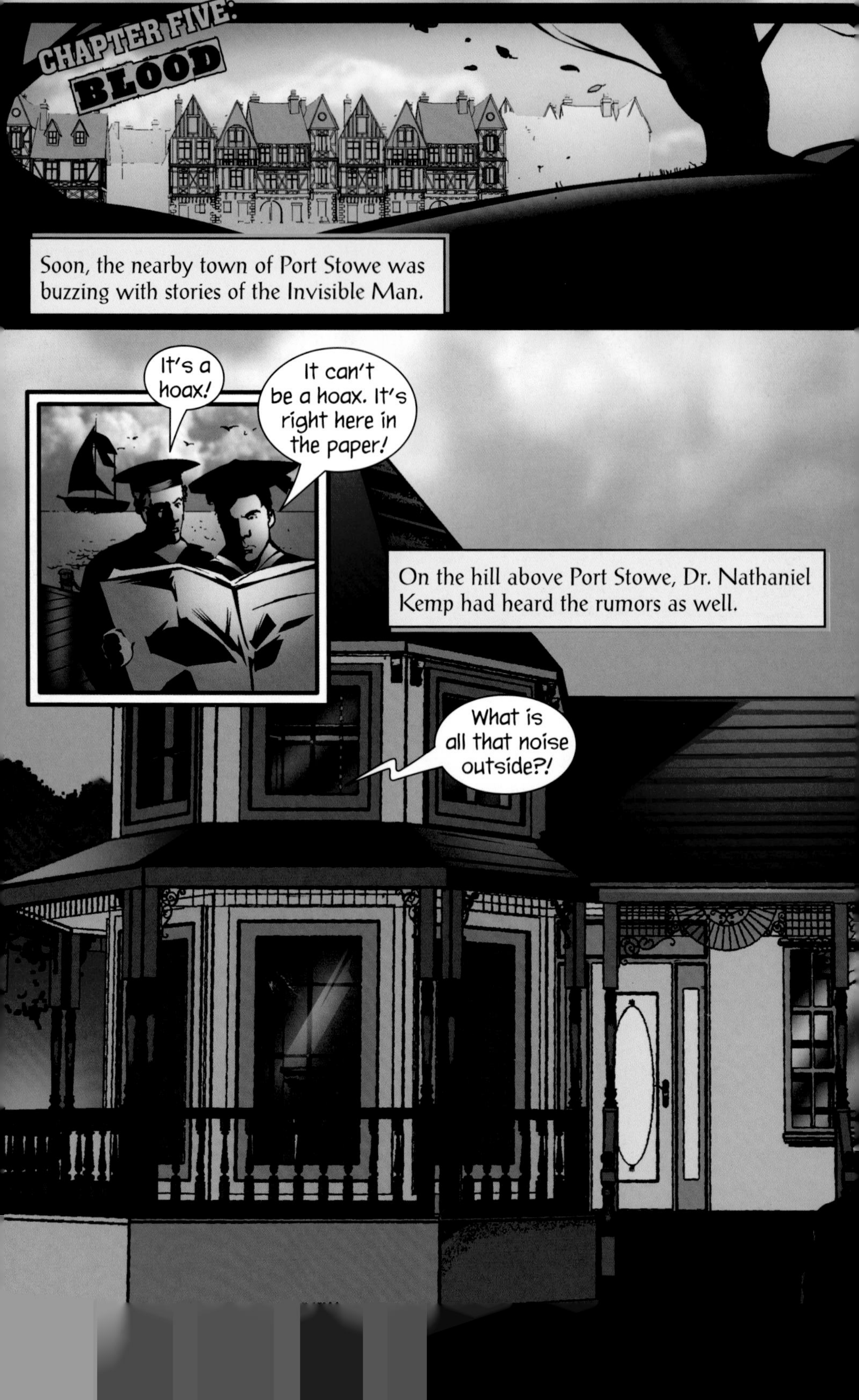
CHAPTER FIVE:
BLOOD
Soon, the nearby town of Port Stowe was buzzing with stories of the Invisible Man.
It's a hoax!
It can't be a hoax. It's right here in the paper!
On the hill above Port Stowe, Dr. Nathaniel Kemp had heard the rumors as well.
What is all that noise outside?!

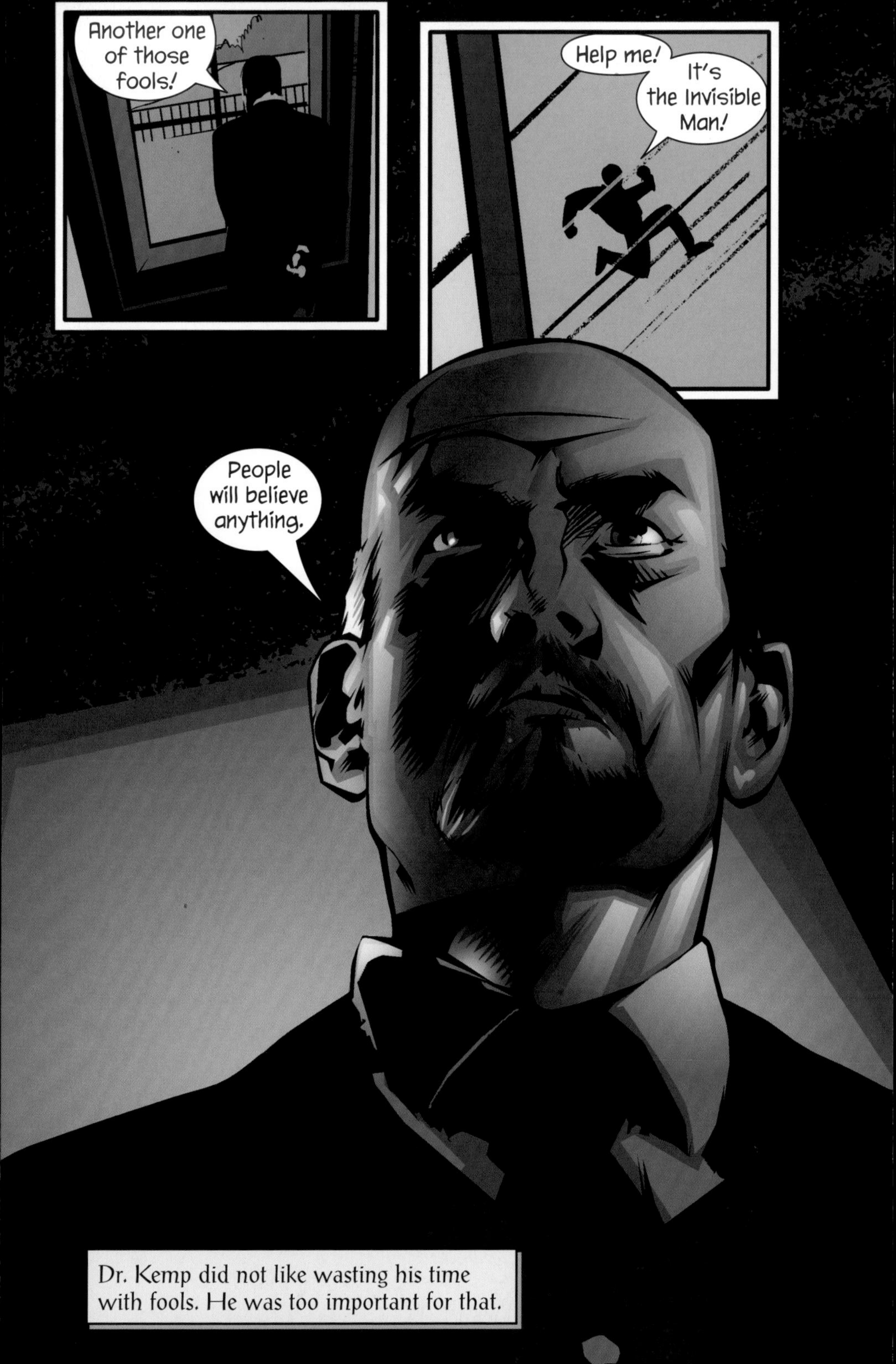
Another one of those fools!
Help me!
It's the Invisible Man!
People will believe anything.
Dr. Kemp did not like wasting his time with fools. He was too important for that.

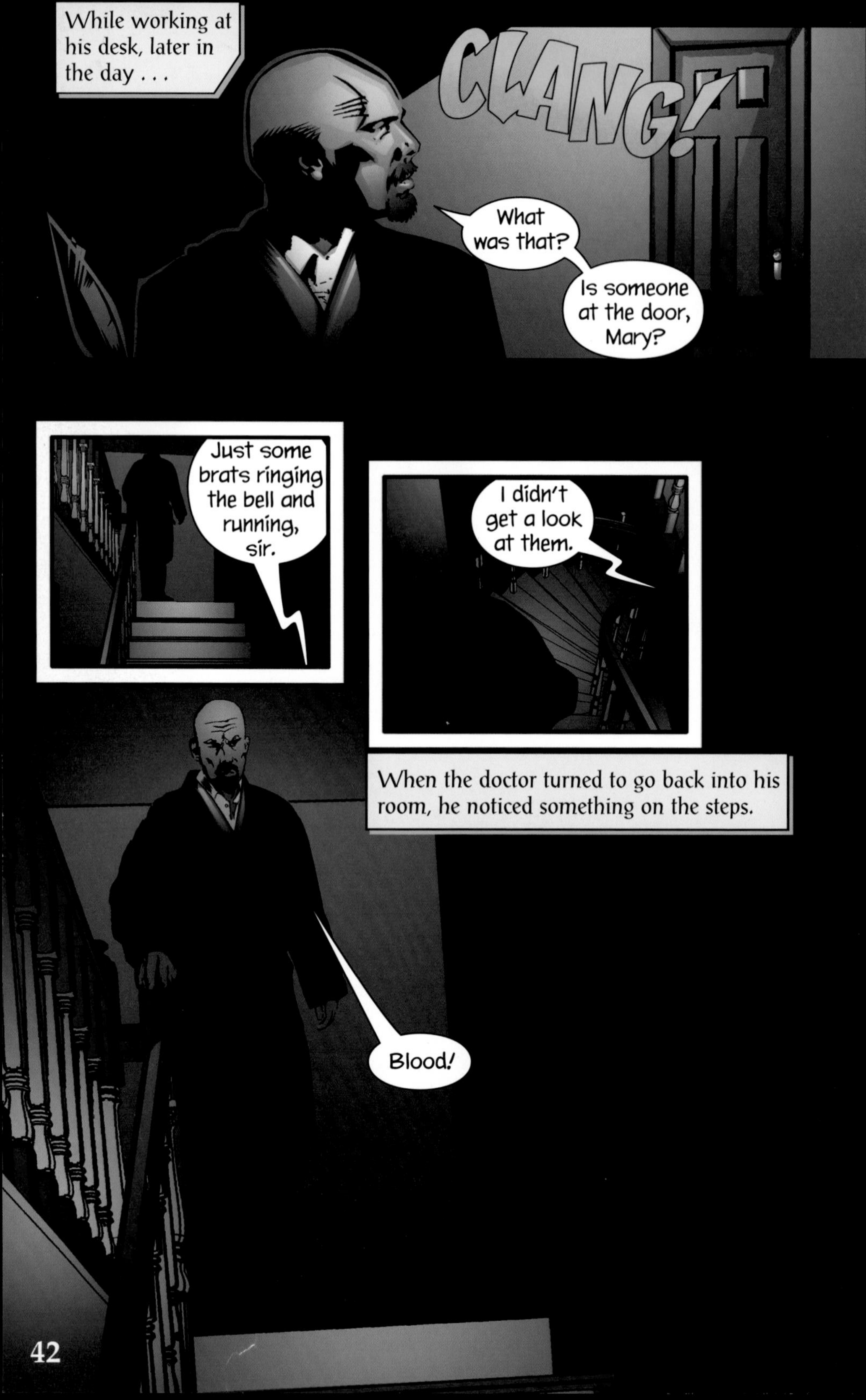
While working at his desk, later in the day . . .
CLANG!
What was that?
Is someone at the door, Mary?
Just some brats ringing the bell and running, sir.
I didn't get a look at them.
When the doctor turned to go back into his room, he noticed something on the steps.
Blood!

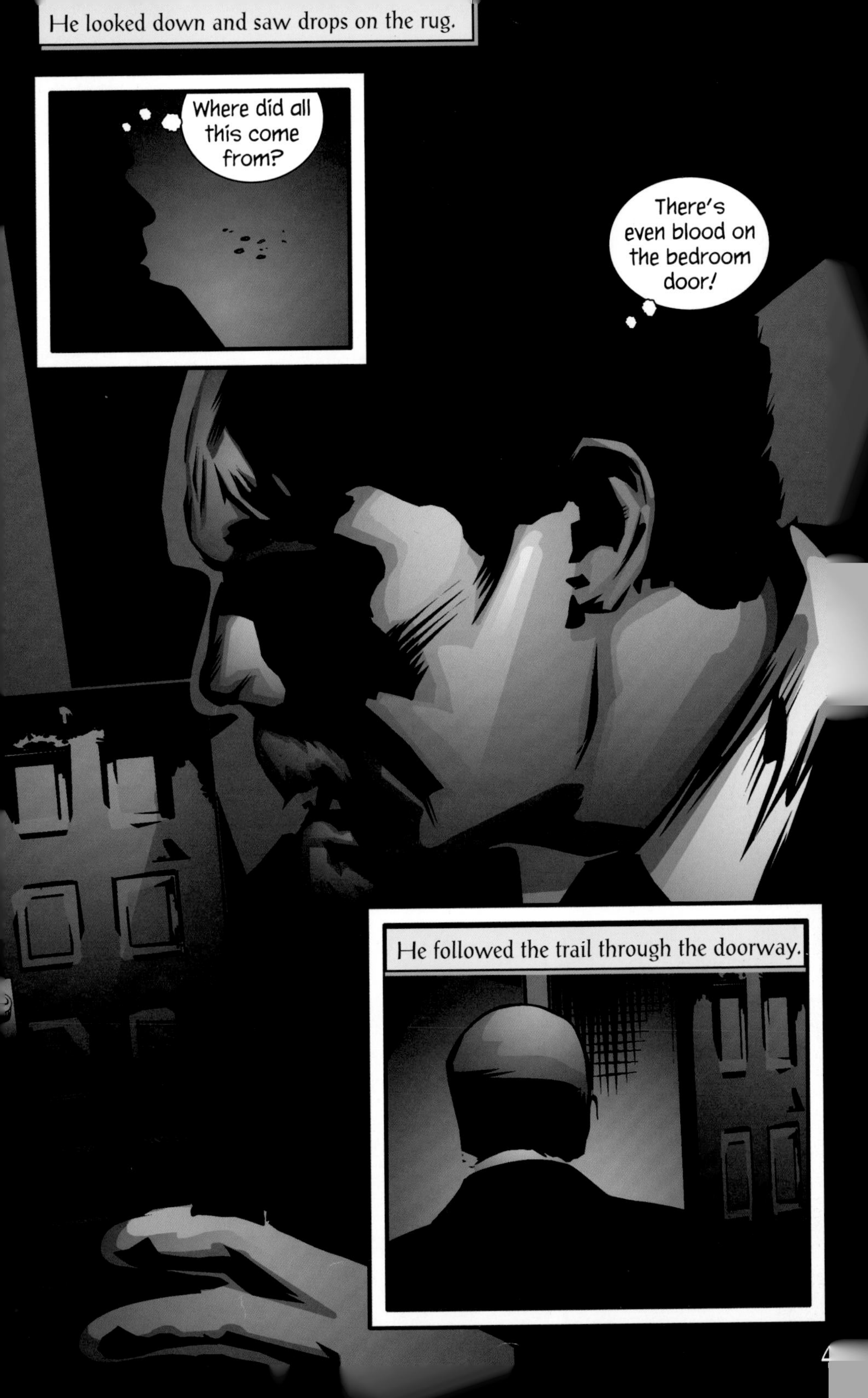
He looked down and saw drops on the rug.
Where did all this come from?
There's even blood on the bedroom door!
He followed the trail through the doorway.

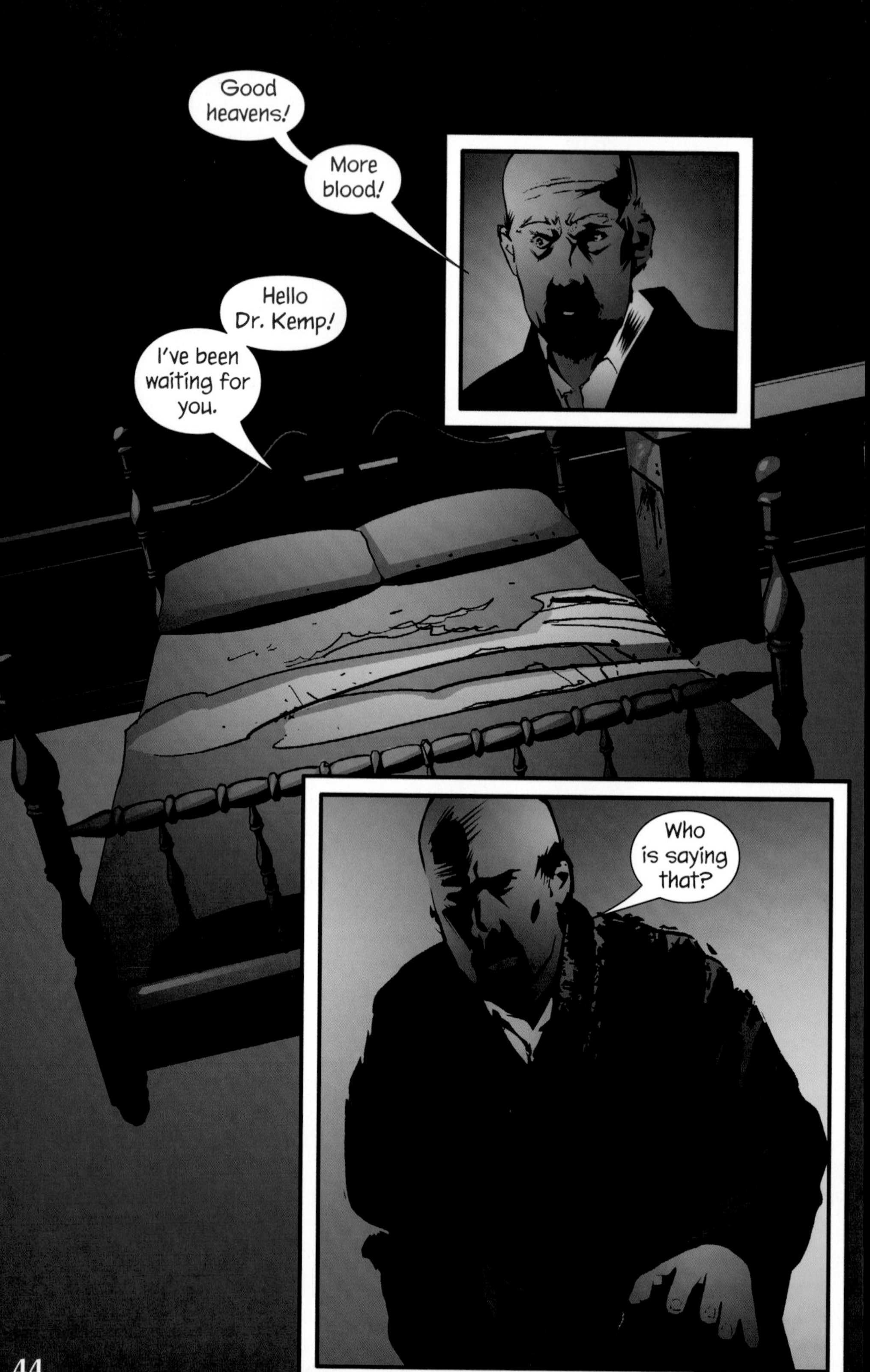
Good heavens!
More blood!
Hello Dr. Kemp!
I've been waiting for you.
Who is saying that?

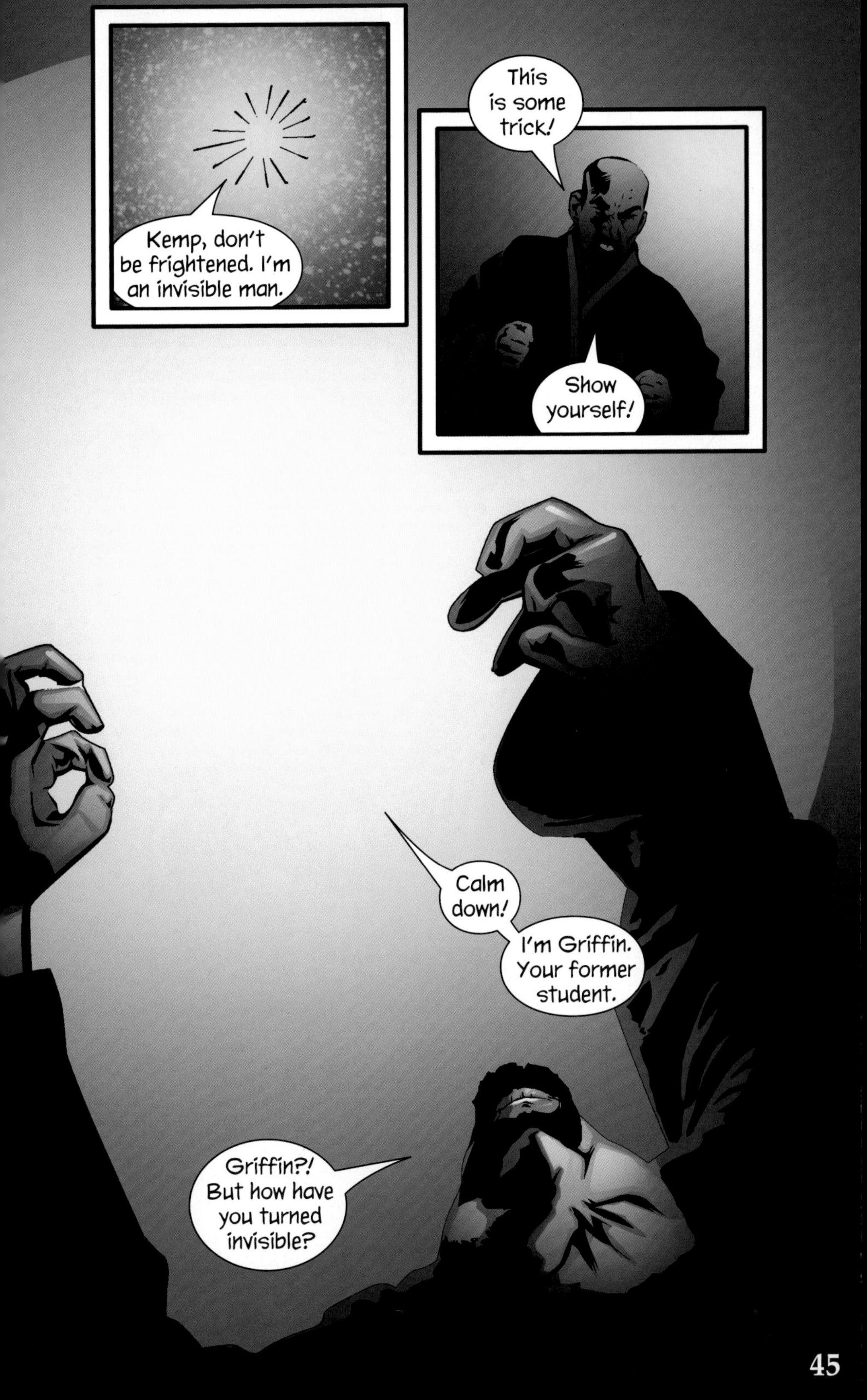

Kemp, don't be frightened. I'm an invisible man.
This is some trick!
Show yourself!
Calm down!
I'm Griffin. Your former student.
Griffin?! But how have you turned invisible?

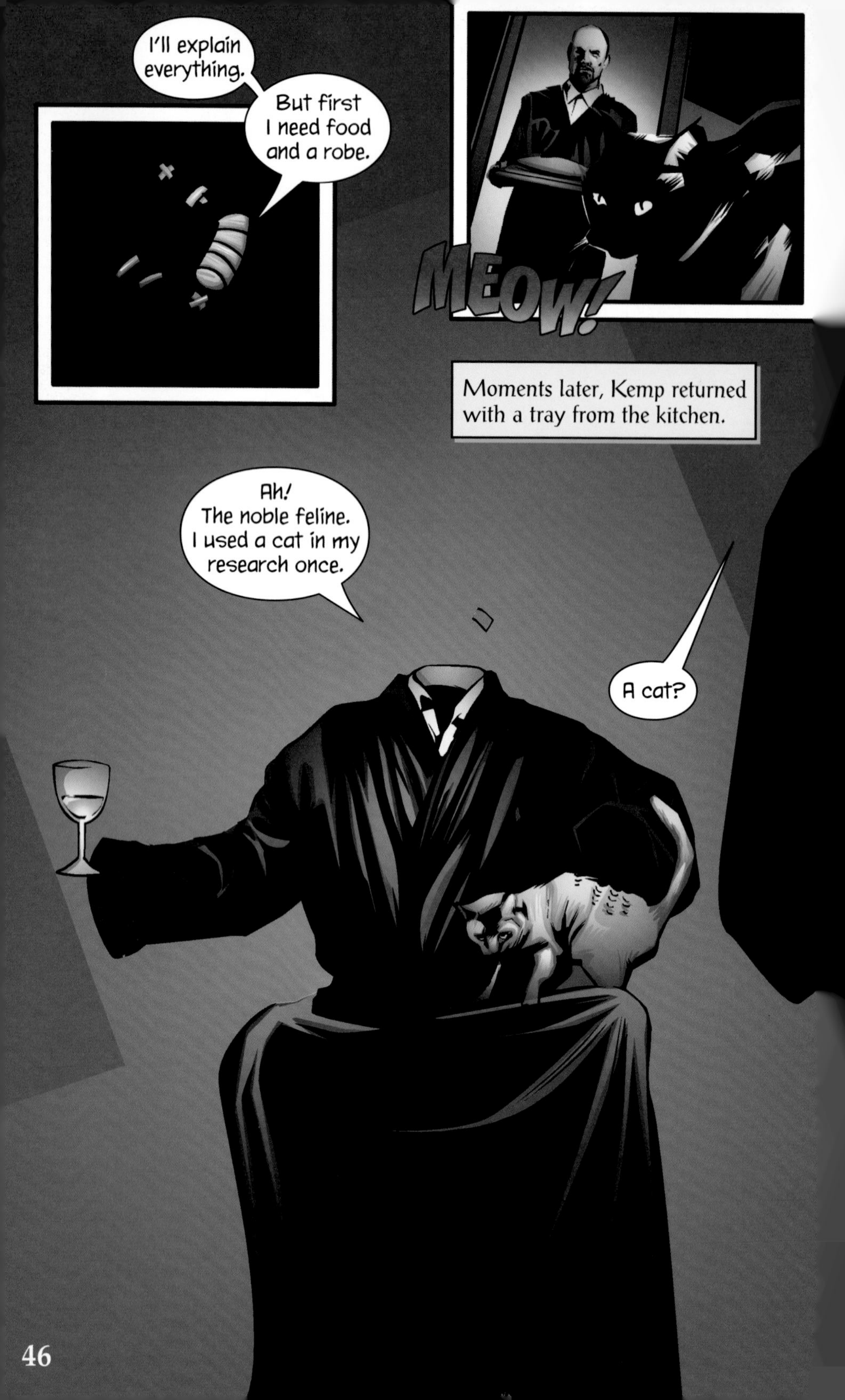
I'll explain everything.
But first I need food and a robe.
MEOW!
Moments later, Kemp returned with a tray from the kitchen.
Ah! The noble feline. I used a cat in my research once.
A cat?

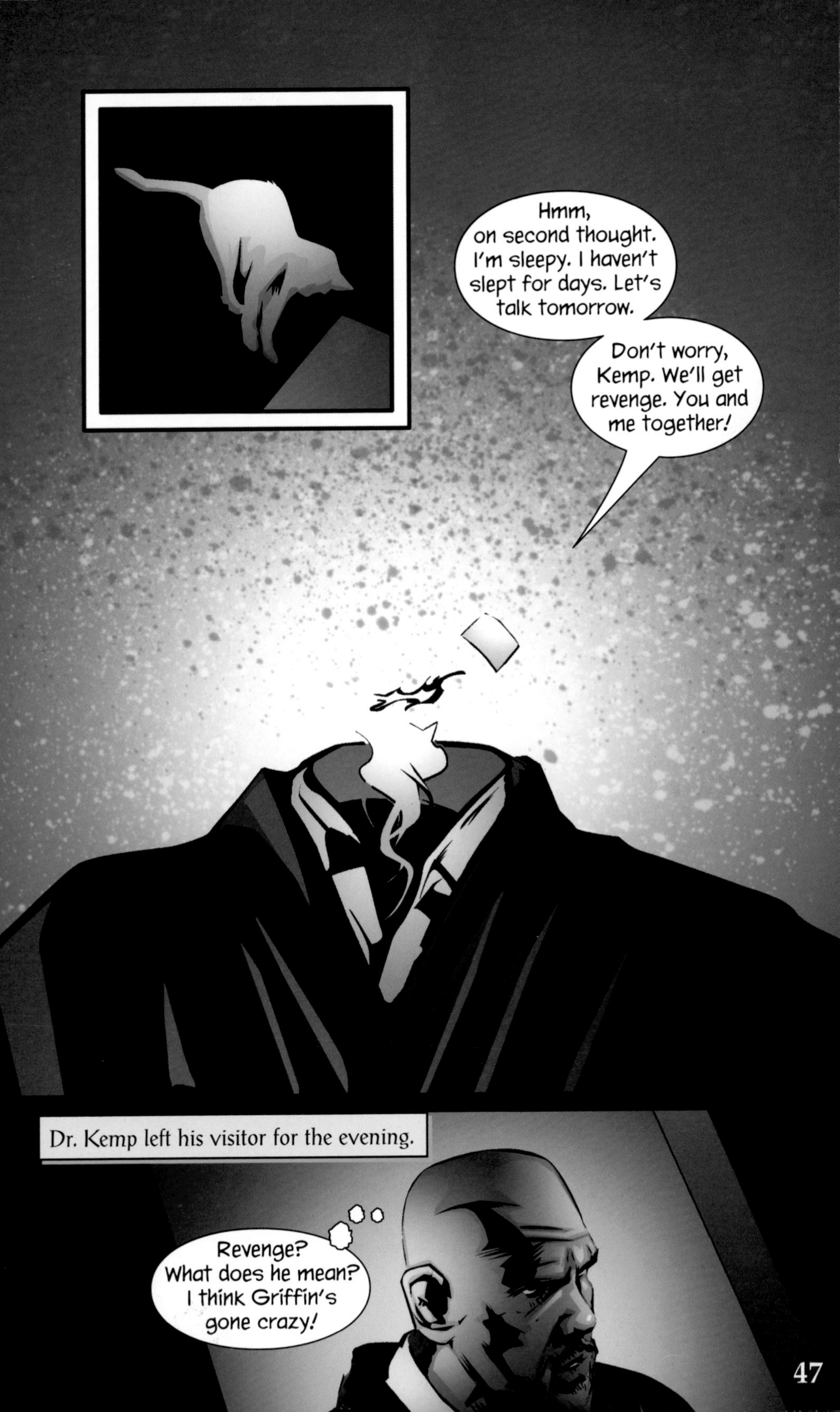

Hmm, on second thought. I'm sleepy. I haven't slept for days. Let's talk tomorrow.
Don't worry, Kemp. We'll get revenge. You and me together!
Dr. Kemp left his visitor for the evening.
Revenge? What does he mean? I think Griffin's gone crazy!

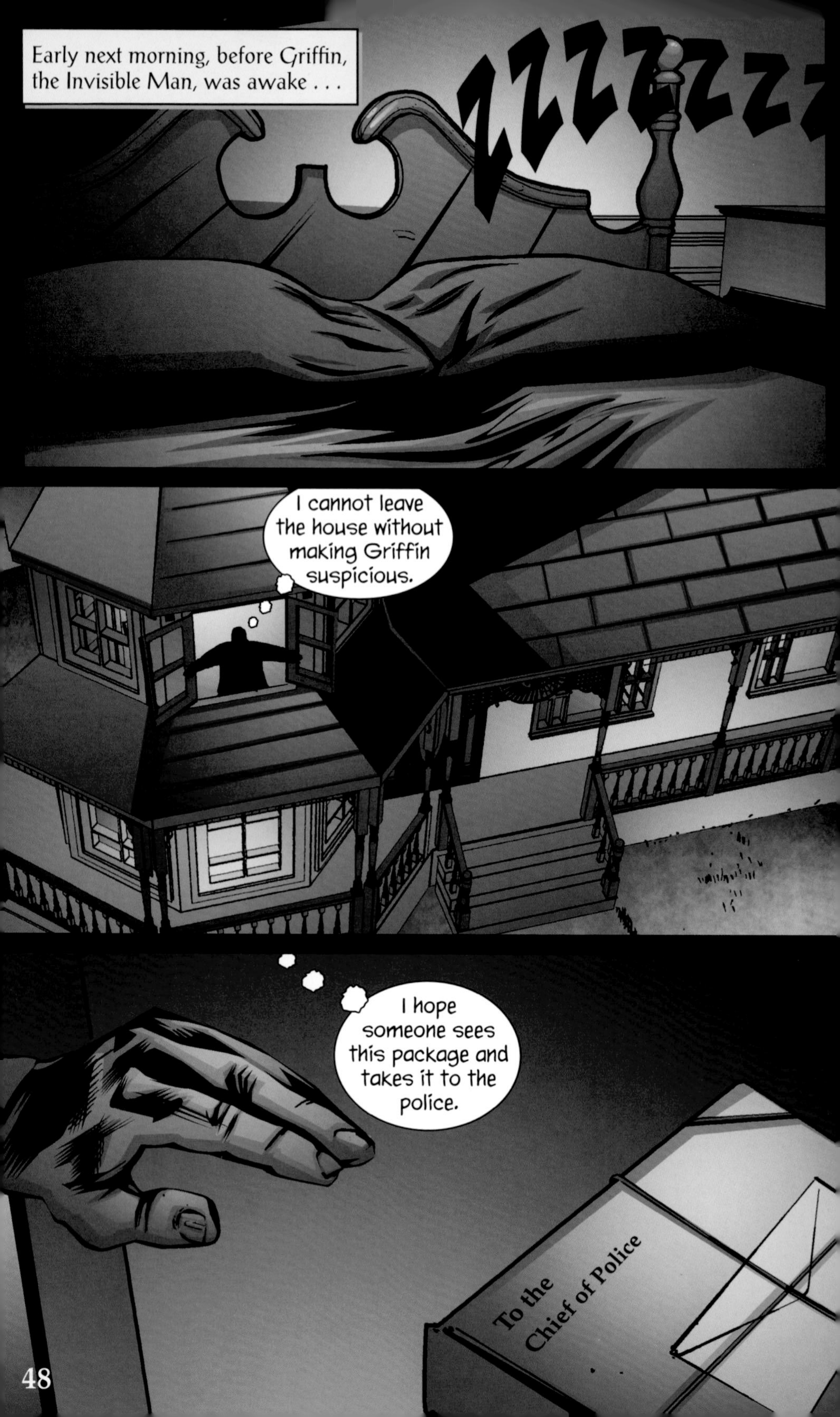
Early next morning, before Griffin, the Invisible Man, was awake . . .
ZZZZZZZ
I cannot leave the house without making Griffin suspicious.
I hope someone sees this package and takes it to the police.
To the Chief of Police

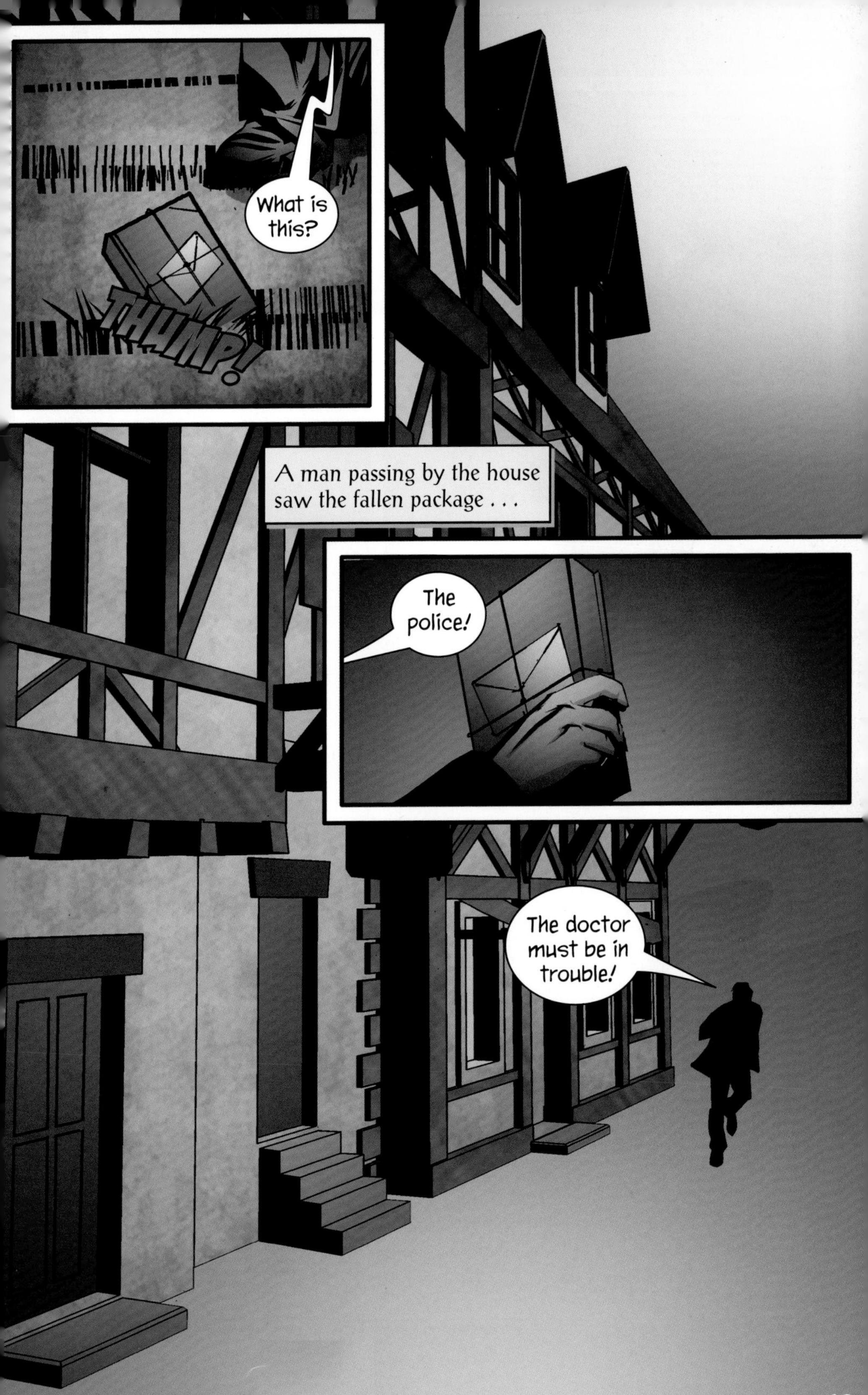
What is this?
THUMP!
A man passing by the house saw the fallen package . . .
The police!
The doctor must be in trouble!

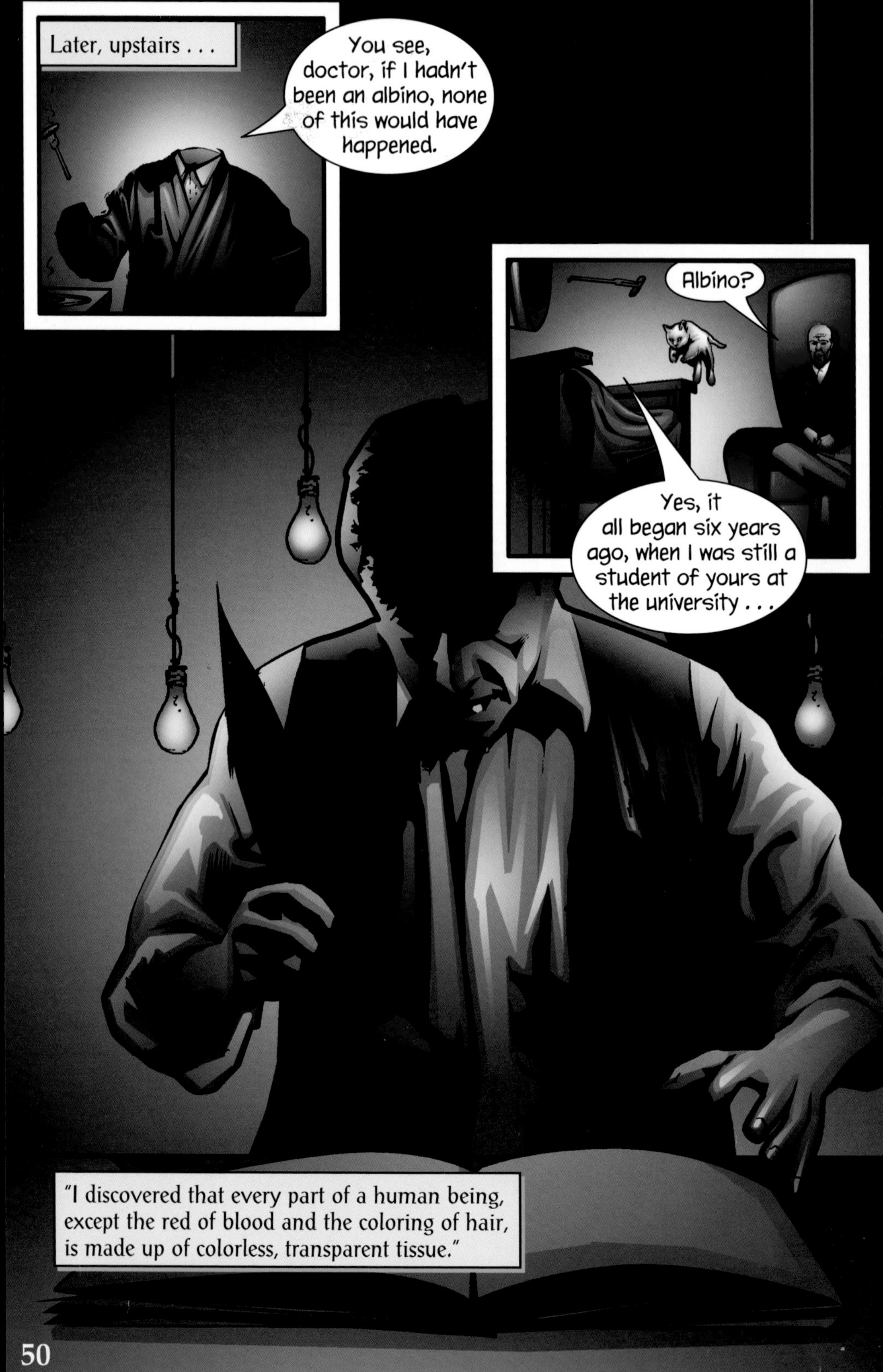
Later, upstairs . . .
You see, doctor, if I hadn't been an albino, none of this would have happened.
Albino?
Yes, it all began six years ago, when I was still a student of yours at the university . . .
"I discovered that every part of a human being, except the red of blood and the coloring of hair, is made up of colorless, transparent tissue."

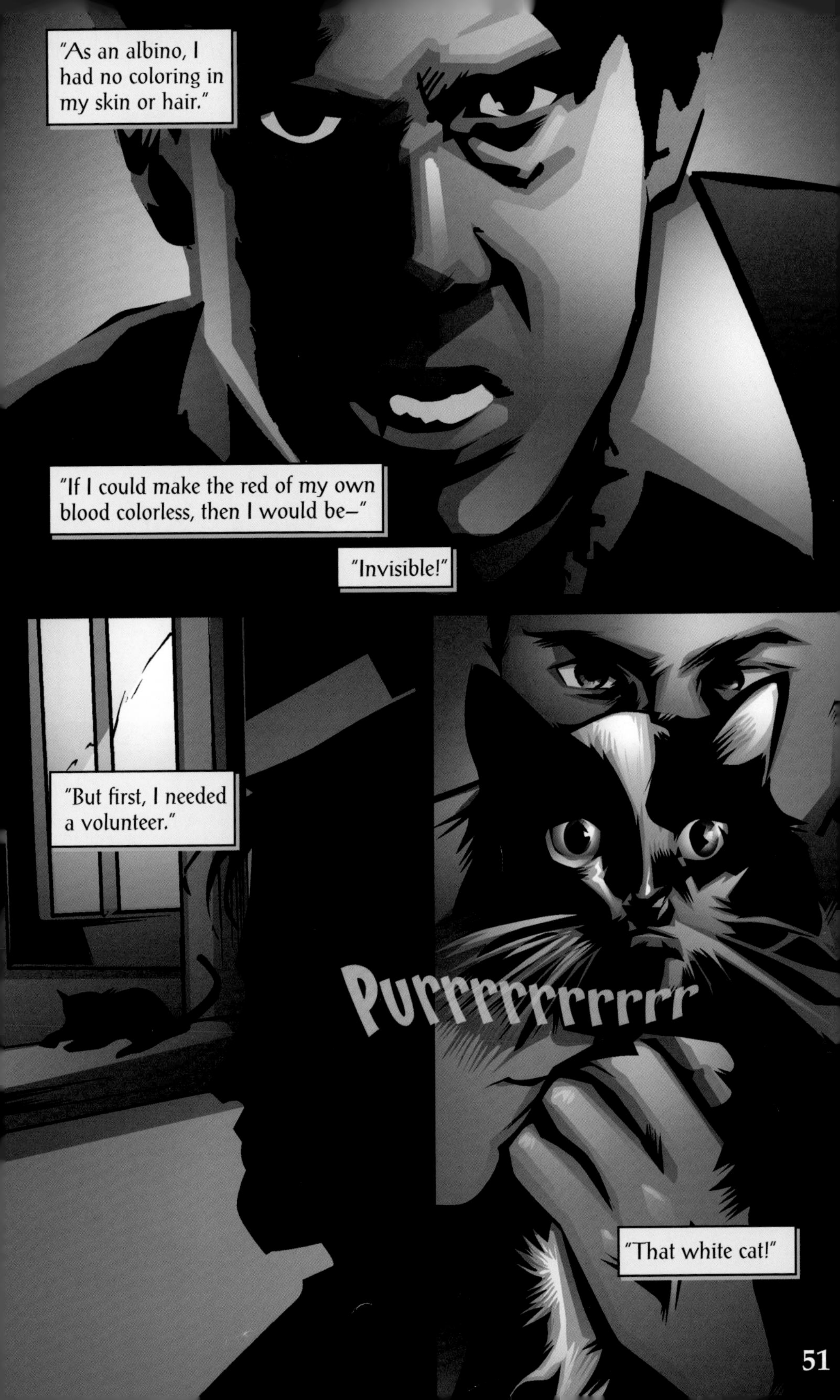
"As an albino, I had no coloring in my skin or hair."
"If I could make the red of my own blood colorless, then I would be–"
"Invisible!"
"But first, I needed a volunteer."
Purrrrrrrrrr
"That white cat!"

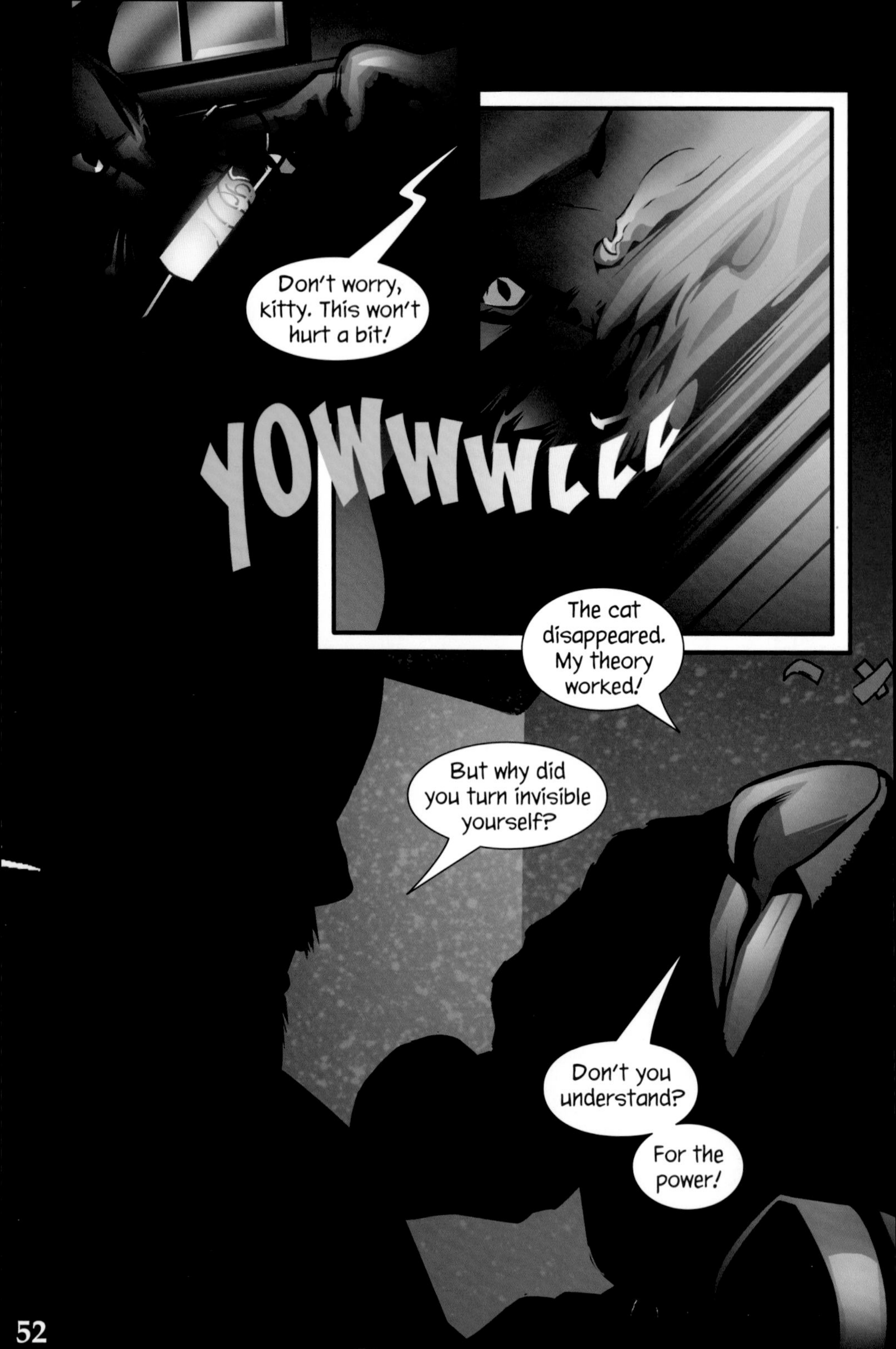
Don't worry, kitty. This won't hurt a bit!
YOWWWLLL
The cat disappeared. My theory worked!
But why did you turn invisible yourself?
Don't you understand?
For the power!

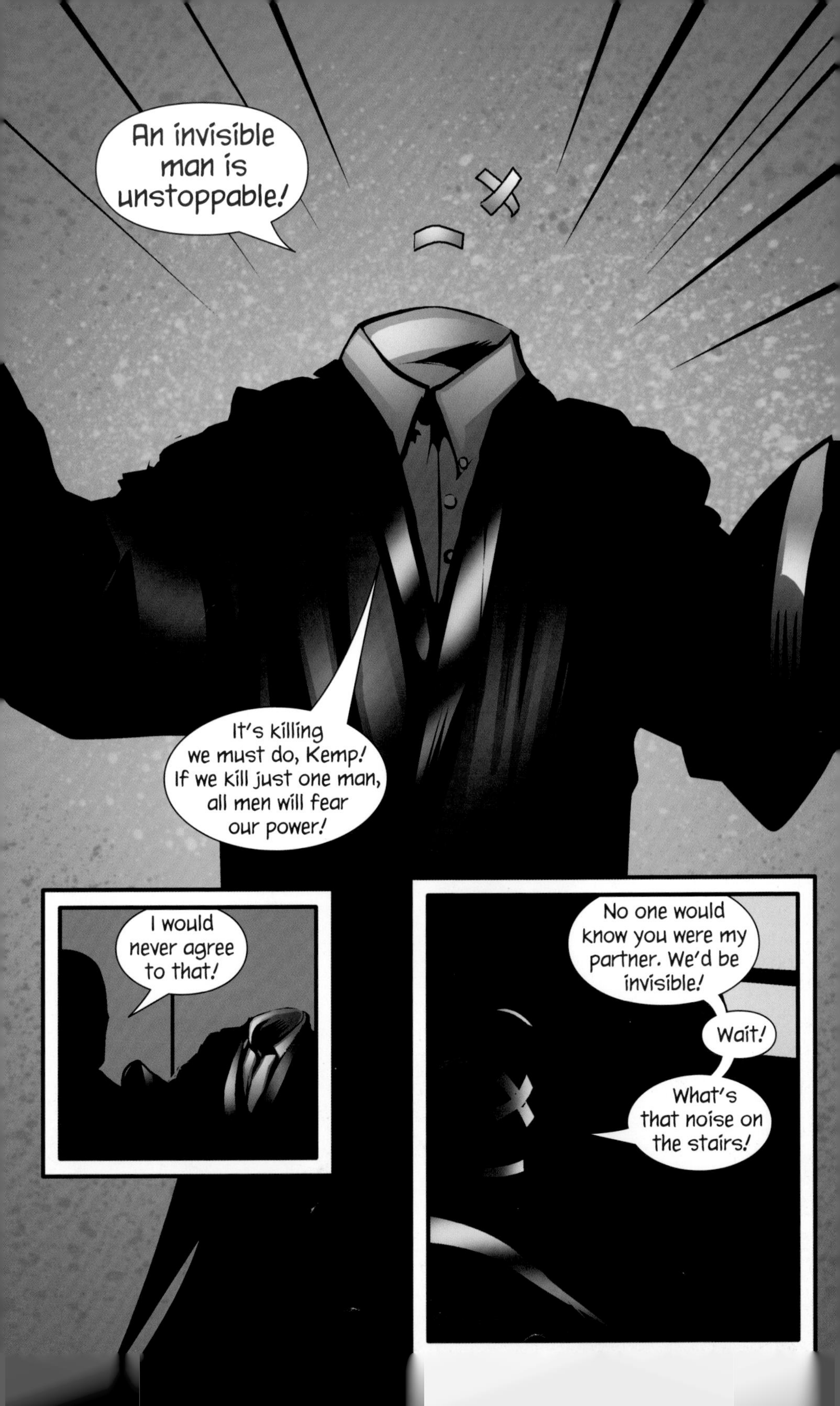
An invisible man is unstoppable!
It's killing we must do, Kemp! If we kill just one man, all men will fear our power!
I would never agree to that!
No one would know you were my partner. We'd be invisible!
Wait!
What's that noise on the stairs!

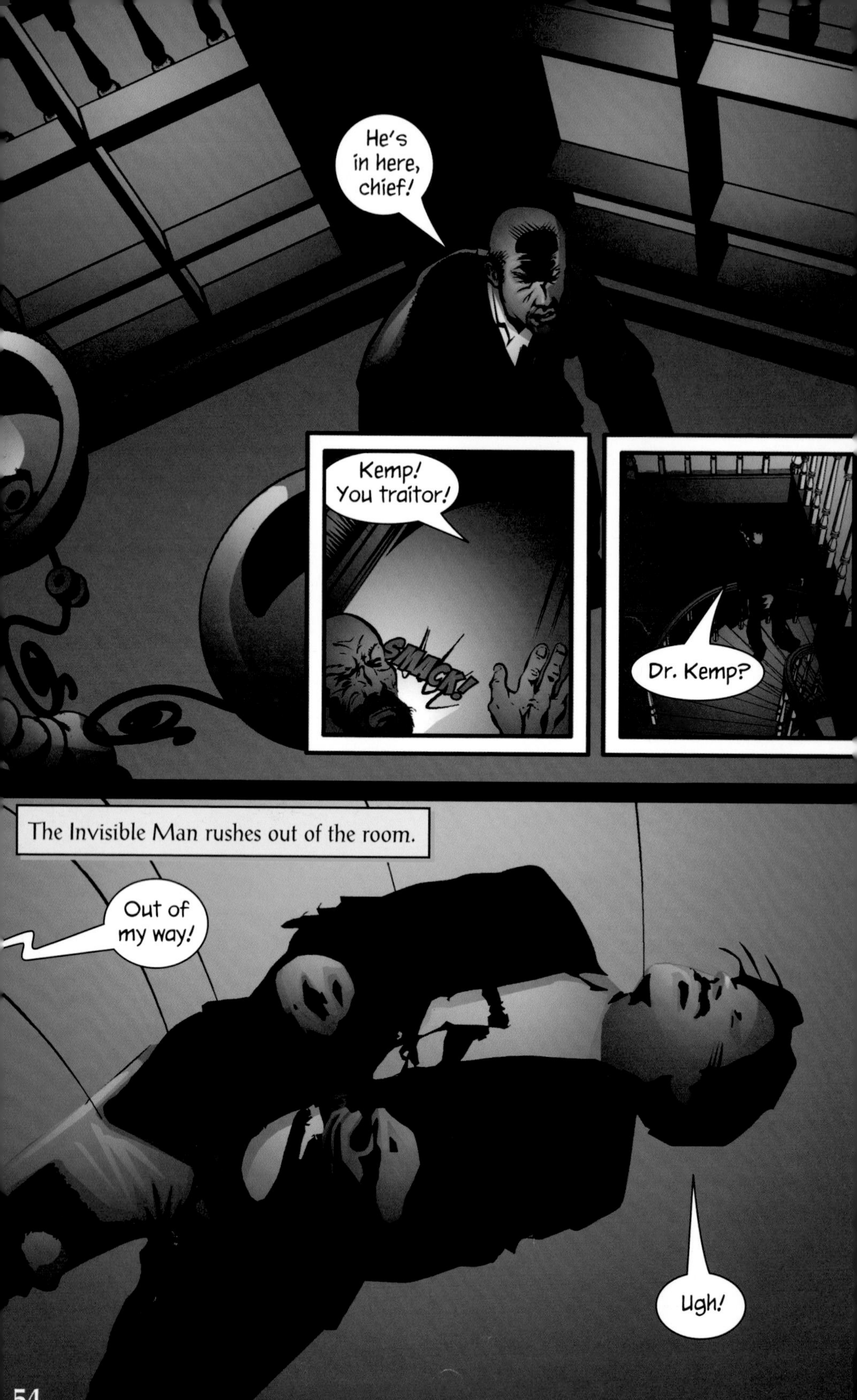
He's in here, chief!
Kemp! You traitor!
SMACK!
Dr. Kemp?
The Invisible Man rushes out of the room.
Out of my way!
Ugh!

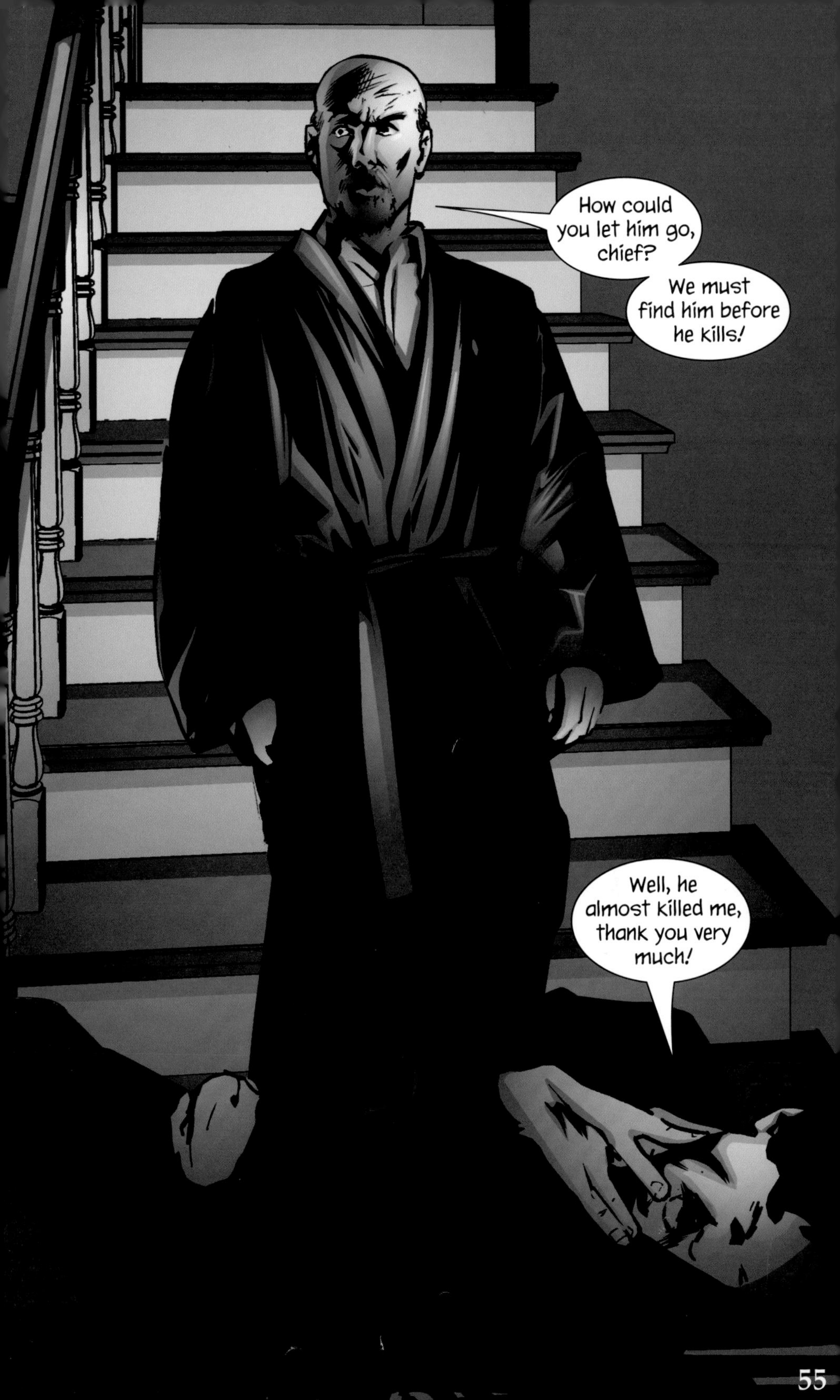
How could you let him go, chief?
We must find him before he kills!
Well, he almost killed me, thank you very much!

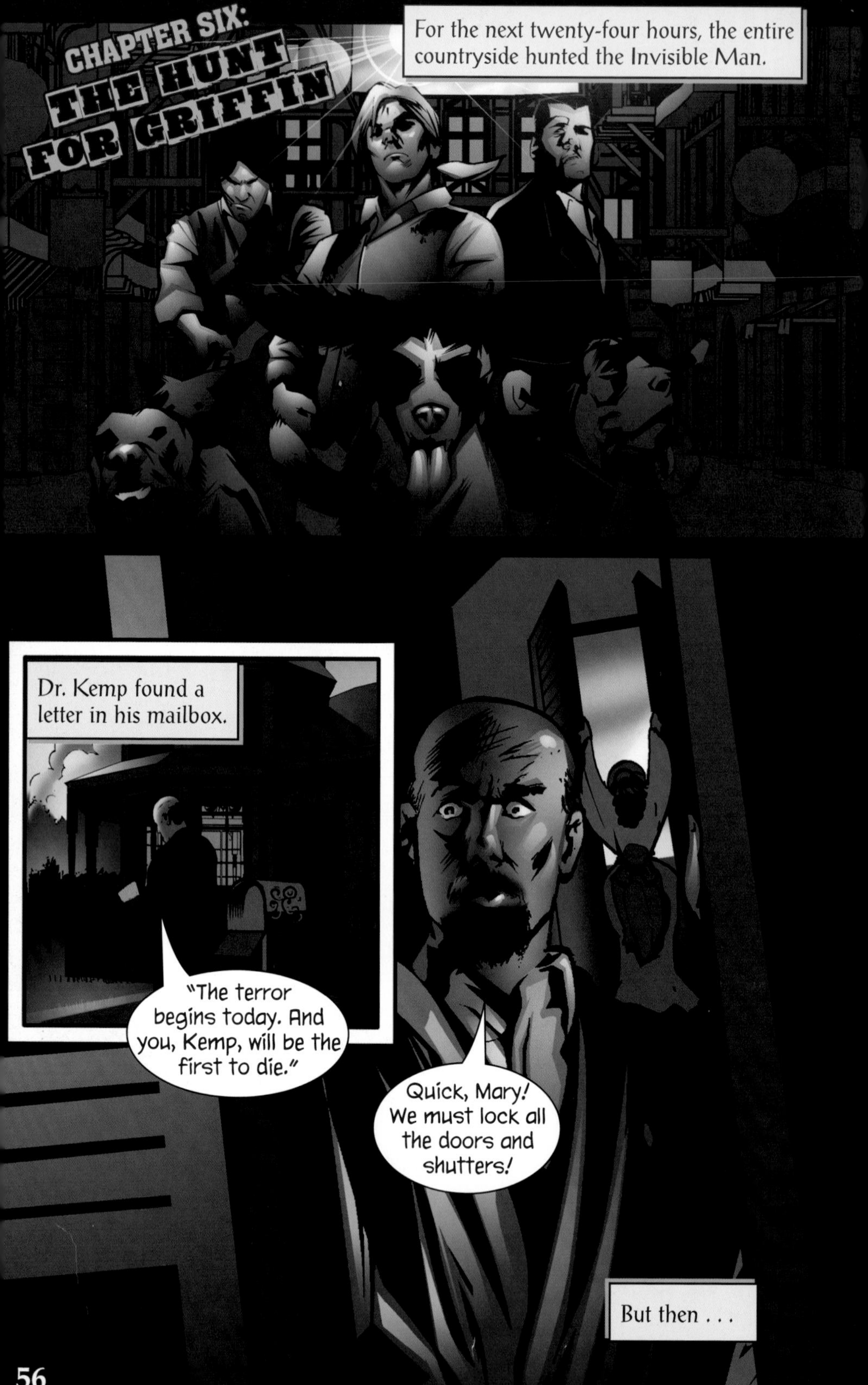

CHAPTER SIX:
THE HUNT FOR GRIFFIN
For the next twenty-four hours, the entire countryside hunted the Invisible Man.
Dr. Kemp found a letter in his mailbox.
"The terror begins today. And you, Kemp, will be the first to die."
Quick, Mary! We must lock all the doors and shutters!
But then . . .

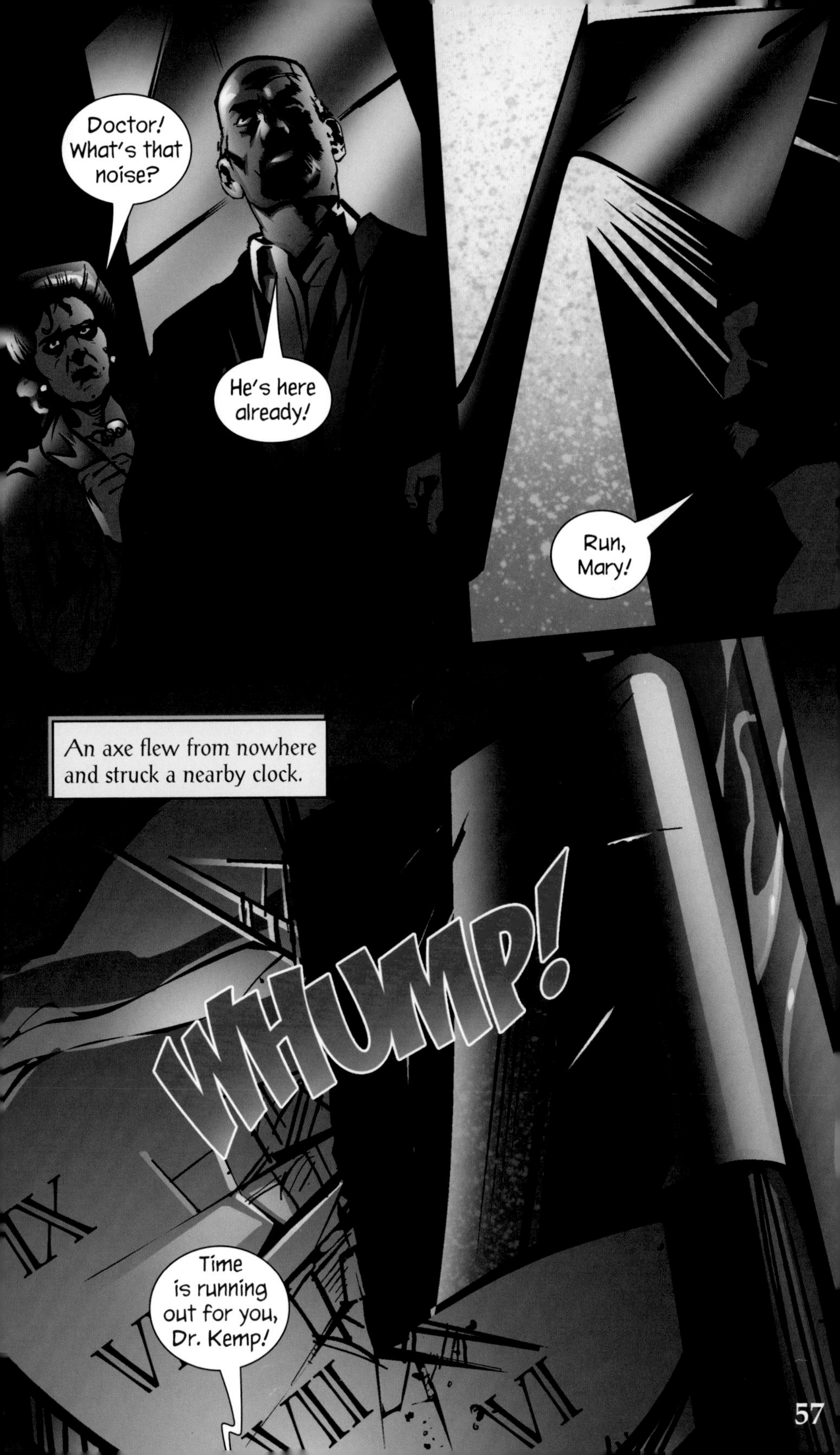
Doctor! What's that noise?
He's here already!
Run, Mary!
An axe flew from nowhere and struck a nearby clock.
WHUMP!
Time is running out for you, Dr. Kemp!

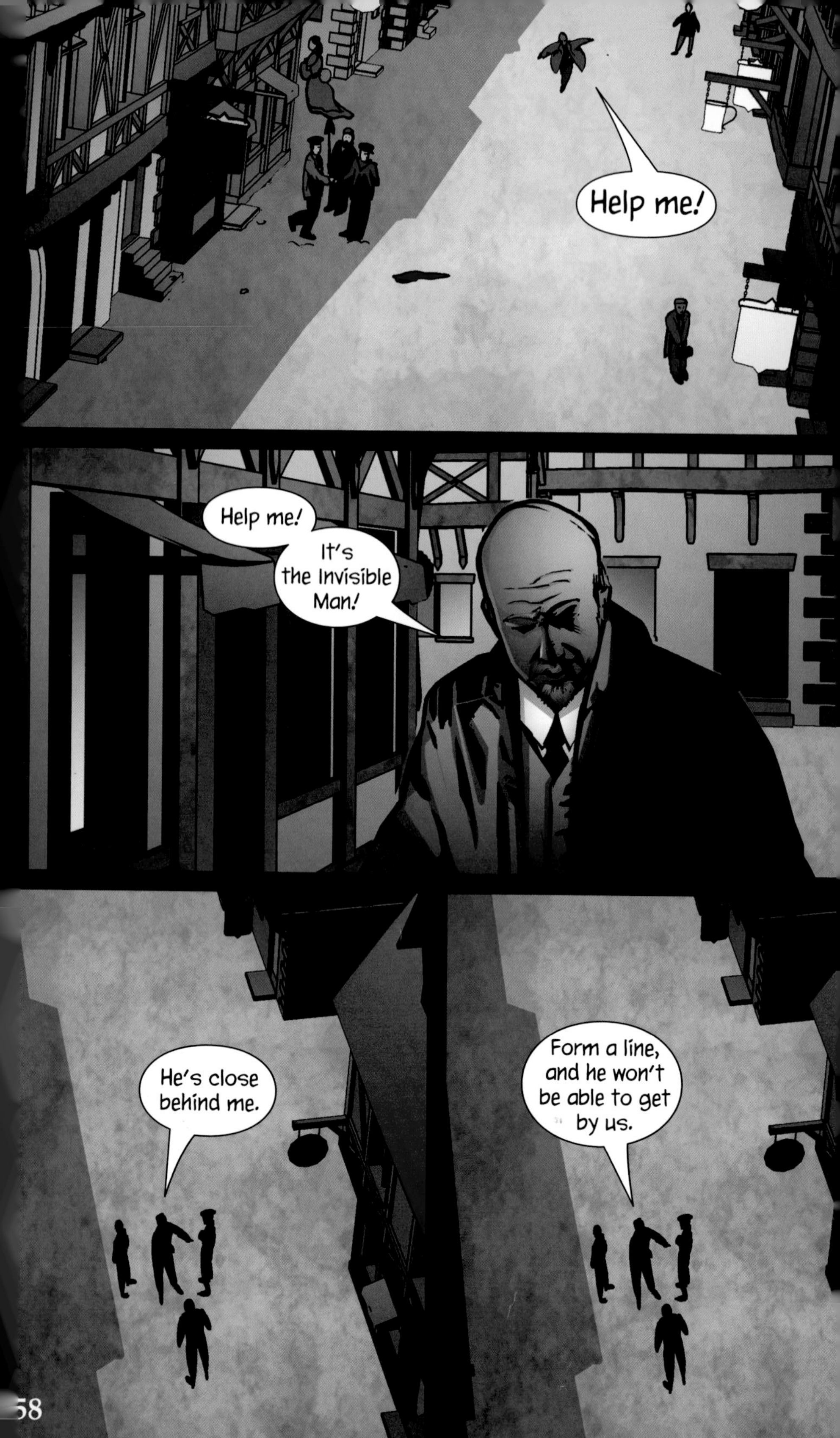
Help me!
Help me!
It's the Invisible Man!
He's close behind me.
Form a line, and he won't be able to get by us.

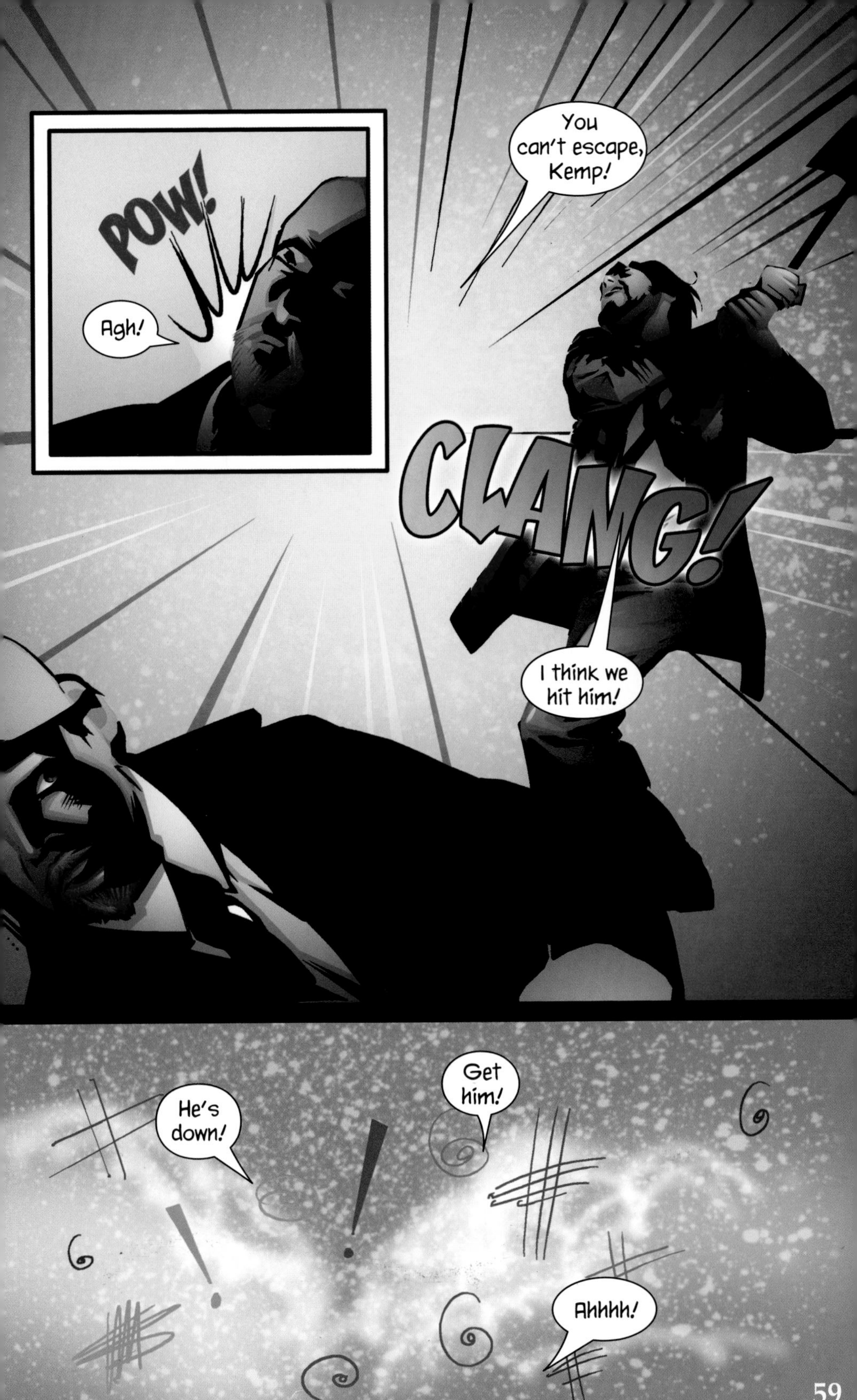
POW!
Agh!
You can't escape, Kemp!
CLANG!
I think we hit him!
He's down!
Get him!
Ahhhh!

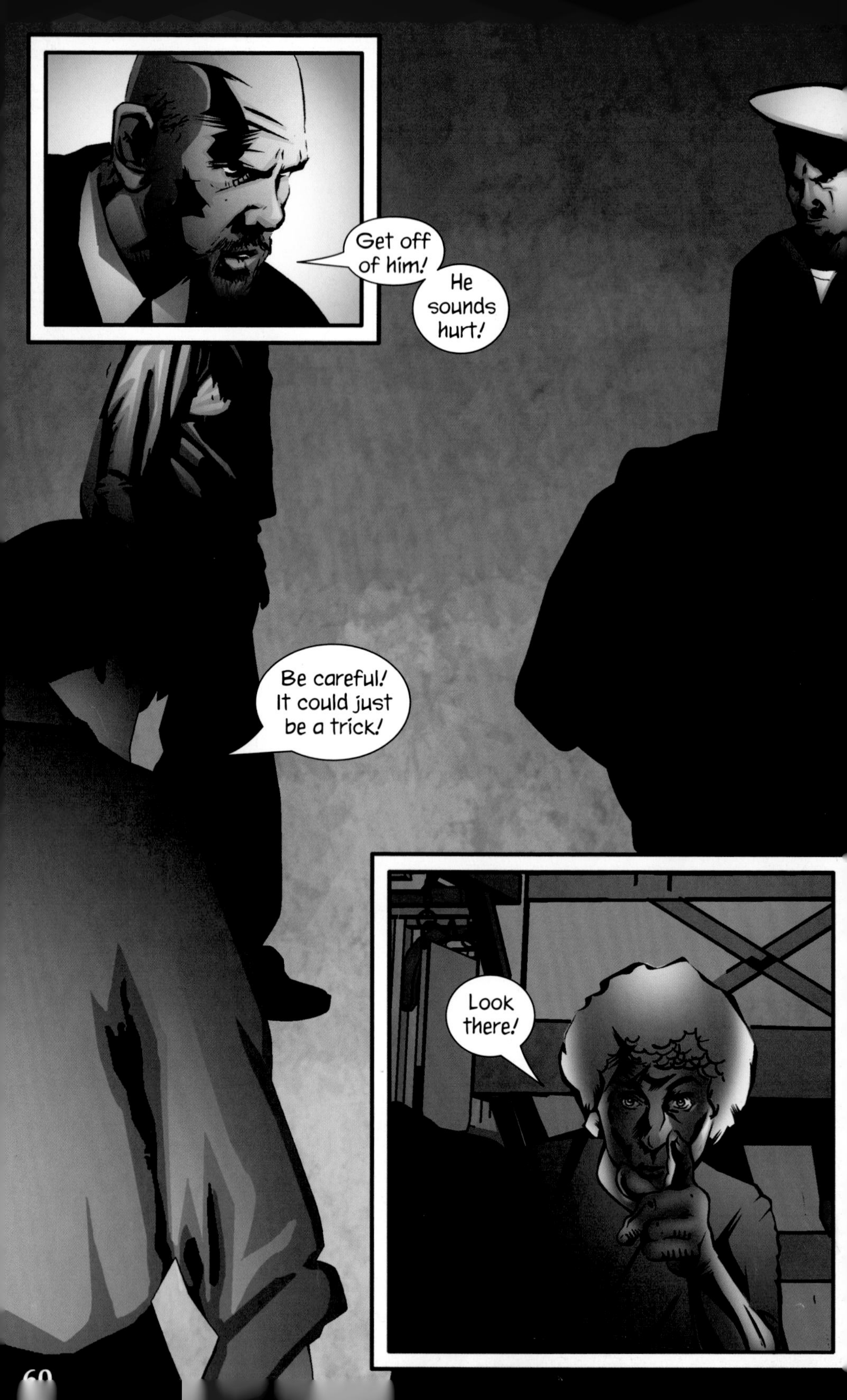
Get off of him!
He sounds hurt!
Be careful! It could just be a trick!
Look there!

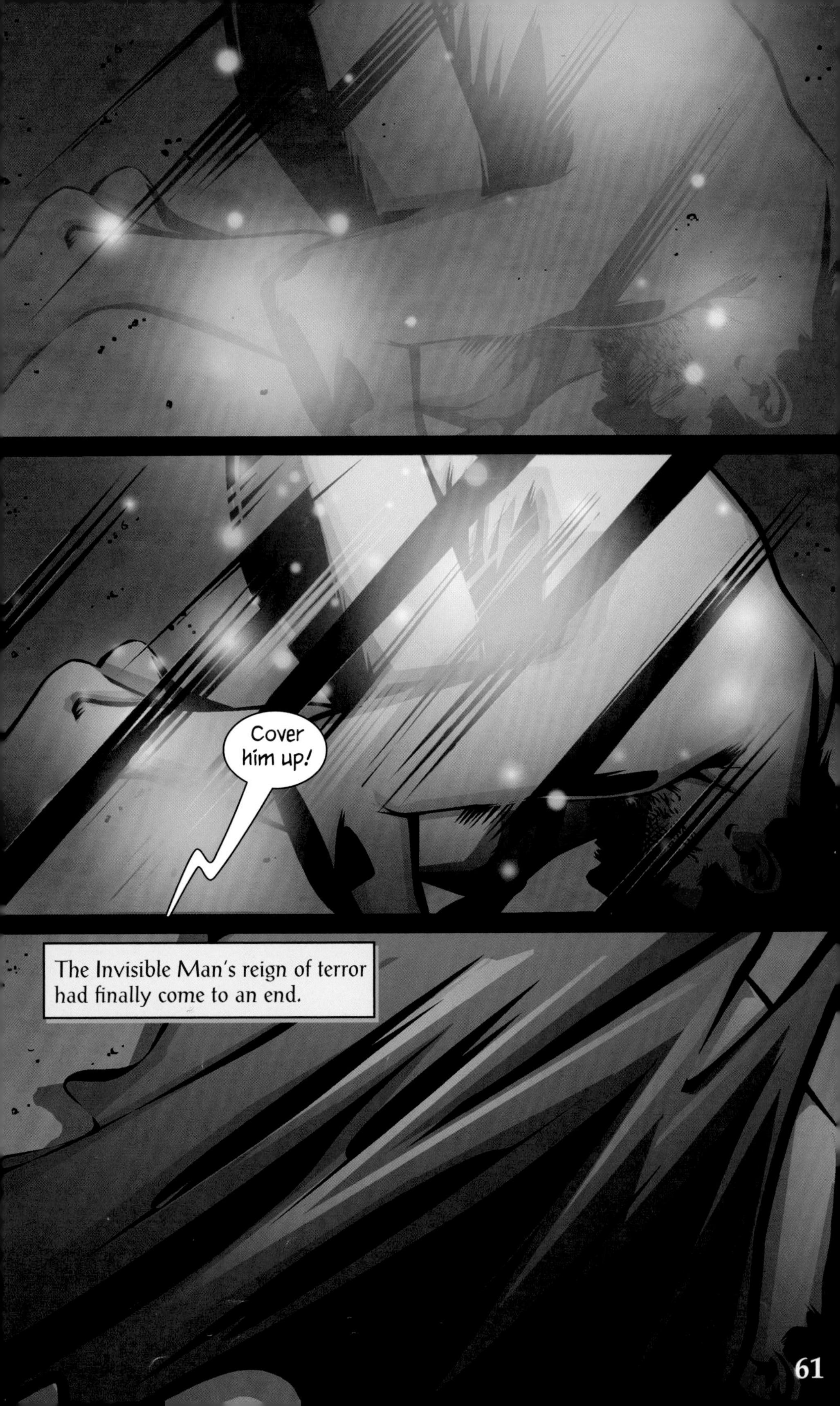
Cover him up!
The Invisible Man's reign of terror had finally come to an end.

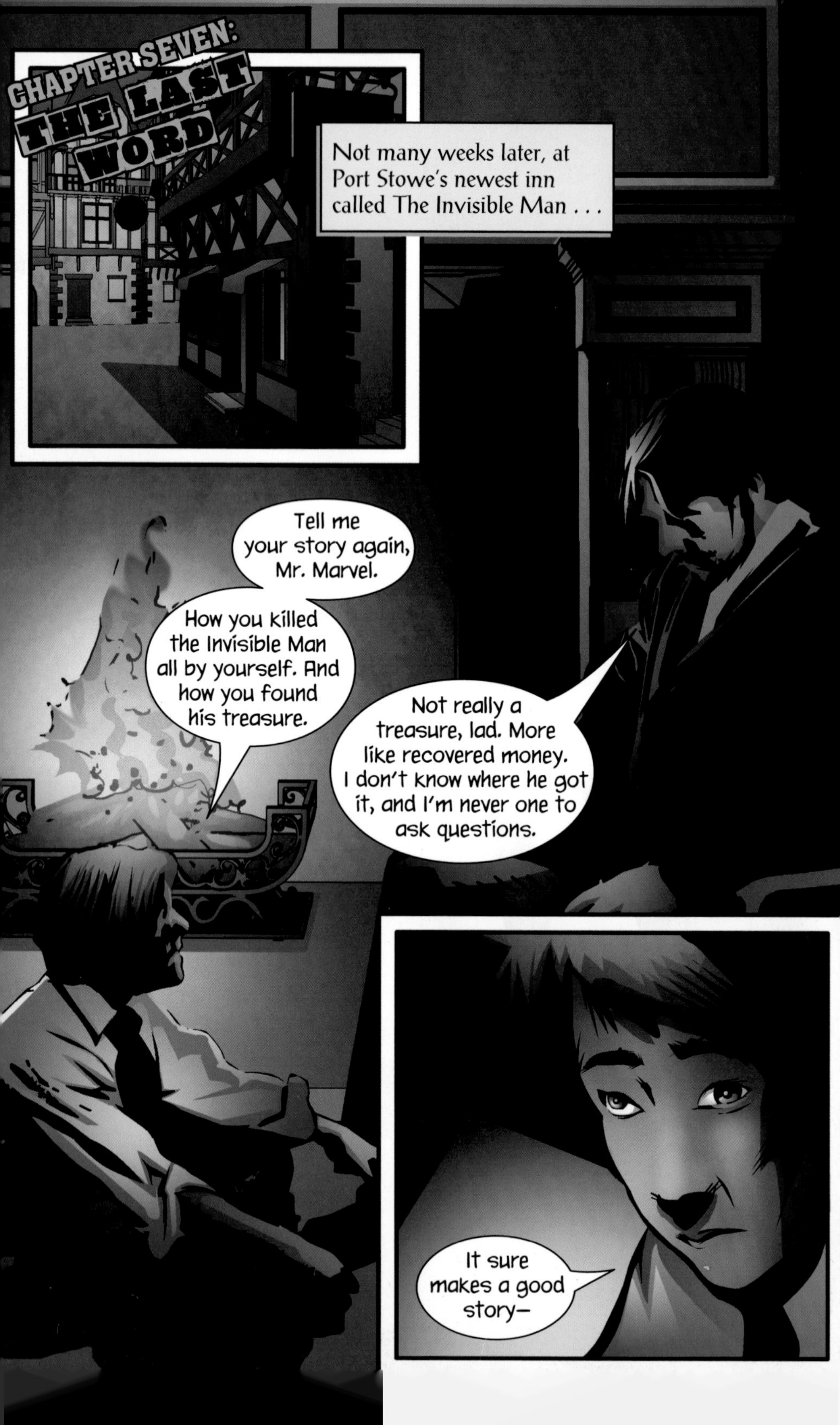
CHAPTER SEVEN:
THE LAST WORD
Not many weeks later, at Port Stowe's newest inn called The Invisible Man . . .
Tell me your story again, Mr. Marvel.
How you killed the Invisible Man all by yourself. And how you found his treasure.
Not really a treasure, lad. More like recovered money. I don't know where he got it, and I'm never one to ask questions.
It sure makes a good story—

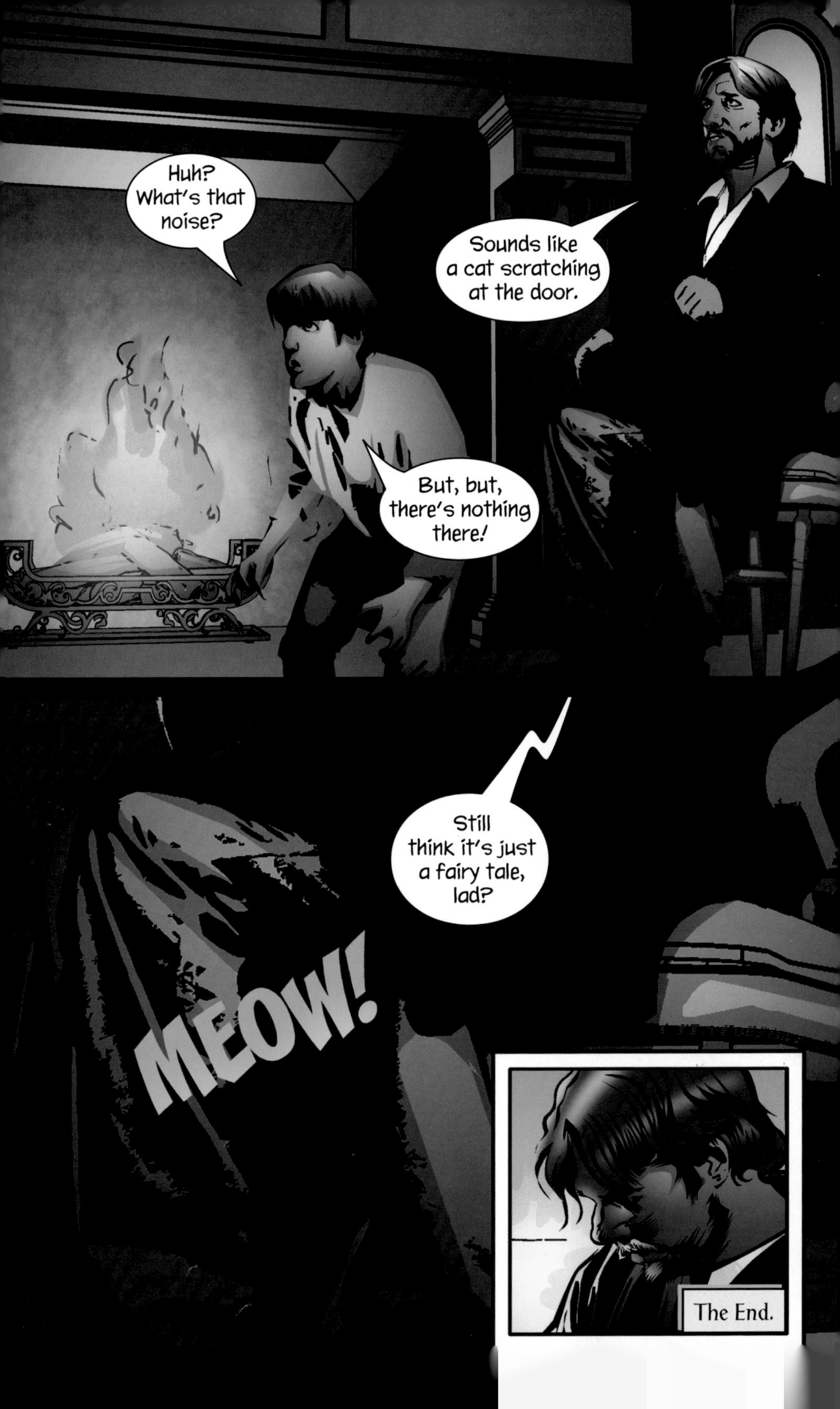
Huh? What's that noise?
Sounds like a cat scratching at the door.
But, but, there's nothing there!
Still think it's just a fairy tale, lad?
MEOW!
The End.

ABOUT H.G. WELLS

Herbert George Wells was born on September 21, 1866, in England. At age 7, he suffered a broken leg. While resting from his injury, Wells started reading books. As he grew older, he continued to enjoy reading and school. At 14, young Wells quit school to help his struggling family. Fortunately, he received a scholarship in 1883 and began studying science at a school in London. Soon after, Wells started writing. Some of his works, like *The Time Machine*, combined his love for storytelling and science. In fact, H.G. Wells is known as one of the first writers of science fiction.

ABOUT THE RETELLING AUTHOR

As a teenager, Terry Davis was a third-string shooting guard for Spokane's Shadle Park High School junior varsity basketball team. In his junior year, Davis turned to wrestling. He took to the sport like a bear to a honeycomb and wrestled his remaining high school years. Today, Davis is a father, a writer, and — in his words — "a fat, old wrestling coach." He also teaches narrative and screenwriting at Minnesota State University, Mankato.

ABOUT THE ILLUSTRATOR

Dennis Calero has illustrated book covers, comic books, and role-playing games for more than ten years. He's worked for companies such as Marvel, DC, White Wolf, and Wizards of the Coast. Dennis is currently illustrating a series of Conan the Barbarian lithographs.

GLOSSARY

albino (al-BY-noh)—a person or animal without any color in their hair, skin, or eyes; albinos are usually white.

druggist (DRUH-gihst)—a person who sells legal medicines or drugs

hoax (HOHKS)—a trick or a joke on someone

inn (IN)—a small hotel, often with a restaurant

reign (RAYN)—a time when someone is in power

shutters (SHUHT-urz)—a moveable cover or screen for a window or door

transparent (transs-PAIR-uhnt)—clear enough to see through, such as glass or some plastics

vicar (VIH-ker)—a member of a church who is in charge of the chapel

victim (VIK-tuhm)—a person that is injured or killed

warrant (WOR-uhnt)—an official document that gives police permission to search for something

THE SCIENCE OF INVISIBILITY

In the story, Griffin invents a potion that turns his blood colorless and makes him invisible. Even before *The Invisible Man* was published, people have searched for ways to disappear. Here are a few facts about invisibility through the years:

Ancient Greeks wrote about the power of invisibility. In one story, a hero named Perseus wore a helmet of invisibility to fight Medusa, an evil monster with snakes for hair. While invisible, Perseus snuck up behind Medusa with his sword and quickly defeated her.

Until the invention of the microscope, many believed fern seeds were invisible. They searched for the seeds, thinking an invisibility potion could be made from enough of them. People eventually realized the seeds were not invisible, just impossible to see with the unaided eye.

Many magicians perform disappearing acts to amaze their audiences. In 1918, famous magician Harry Houdini made an elephant vanish. In 1984, David Copperfield made the Statue of Liberty disappear on national TV.

For years, military experts have searched for ways to make them invisible to their enemies. In the early 1900s, camouflage uniforms became popular and helped soldiers "disappear" into their surroundings. Later, scientists developed stealth (STELTH) technology, a design that makes an airplane nearly invisible to radar.

Modern storytellers continue to imagine the possibilities of being invisible. In *Lord of the Rings* by J. R. R. Tolkien, anyone wearing a powerful ring becomes invisible. Author J. K. Rowling gave her main character, Harry Potter, an invisibility cloak for protection.

Scientists in the United States and Great Britain are working on inventing a real "invisibility cloak." This cloak, however, would only hide objects from radar.

DISCUSSION QUESTIONS

1. Dr. Nathaniel Kemp was the Invisible Man's friend, but he turned him in to the police. Why do you think Kemp told on his friend? Would you ever tell on your friend for doing something wrong? Why or why not?

2. Why do you think the Invisible Man was so evil? Do you think he became mean because of the way people treated him? Explain your answer using some examples from the story.

3. People often wish for something without thinking about both the pros and the cons. Griffin dreamed of becoming invisible, but he didn't consider the disadvantages. Discuss some of the advantages and disadvantages of being invisible.

4. At the end of the story, the Invisible Man dies. Do you feel sorry for the Invisible Man, or do you think he deserved what happened? Explain your answer.

WRITING PROMPTS

1. Griffin, the Invisible Man, commits a lot of crimes because he believes no one can catch him. List three ways that you would have captured Griffin. Write a new ending to the story using one of your plans.

2. Imagine that you could become invisible for 24 hours. Describe where you would go and what you would do on that day.

3. Being invisible is like having a superpower. If you could choose any superpower, what would it be? Would you want to fly? How about X-ray vision? Pick a superpower, and describe what you would do with this special ability.

OTHER BOOKS

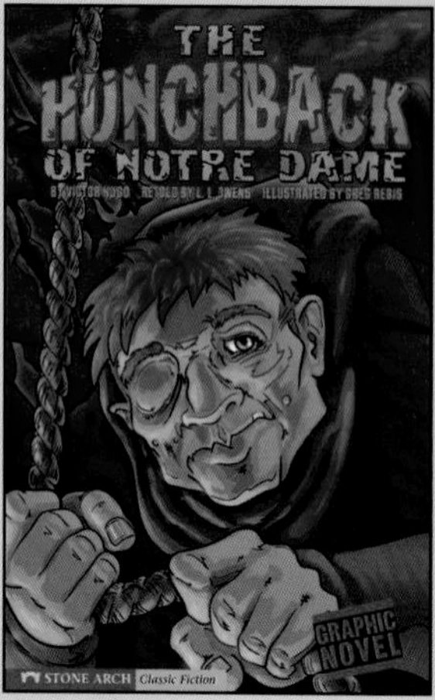
THE HUNCHBACK OF NOTRE DAME
GRAPHIC NOVEL
STONE ARCH Classic Fiction

The Hunchback of Notre Dame

Hidden away in the bell tower of the Cathedral of Notre Dame, Quasimodo is treated like a beast. Although he is gentle and kind, he has the reputation of a frightening monster because of his physical deformities. He develops affection for Esmeralda, a gypsy girl who shows him kindness in return. When the girl is sentenced to an unfair death by hanging, Quasimodo is determined to save her. But those closest to Quasimodo have other plans for the gypsy.

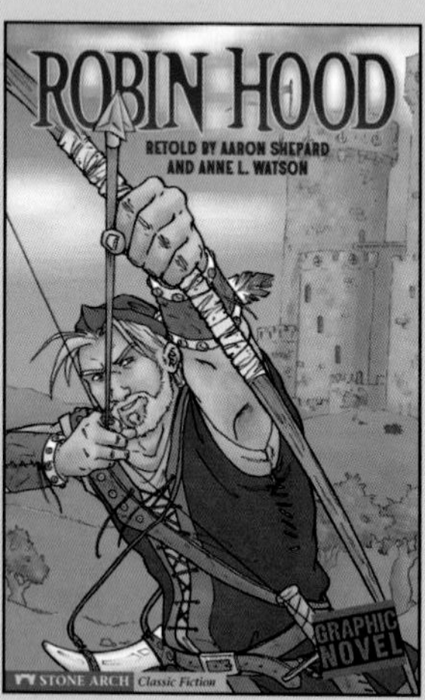
ROBIN HOOD
RETOLD BY AARON SHEPARD AND ANNE L. WATSON
GRAPHIC NOVEL
STONE ARCH Classic Fiction

Robin Hood

Robin Hood and his Merrie Men are the heroes of Sherwood Forest. Taking from the rich and giving to the poor, Robin Hood and his loyal followers fight for the downtrodden and oppressed. As they outwit the cruel Sheriff of Nottingham, Robin Hood and his Merrie Men are led on a series of exciting adventures.

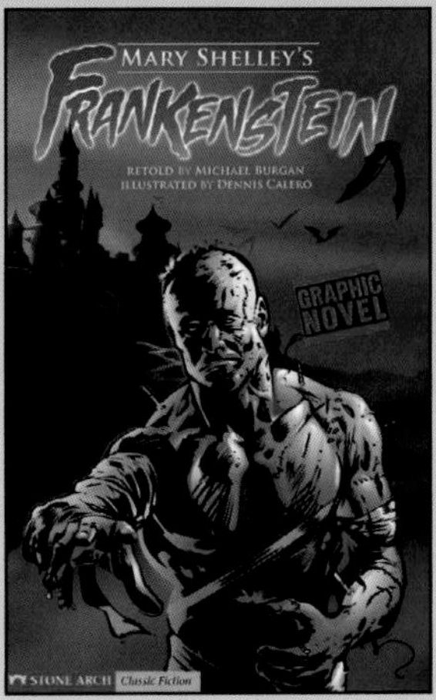
MARY SHELLEY'S
FRANKENSTEIN
RETOLD BY MICHAEL BURGAN
ILLUSTRATED BY DENNIS CALERO
GRAPHIC NOVEL
STONE ARCH
Classic Fiction

Frankenstein

The young scientist Victor Frankenstein has created something amazing and horrible at the same time — a living being out of dead flesh and bone. His creation, however, turns out to be a monster! Frankenstein's creation quickly discovers that his hideous appearance frightens away any companions. Now Victor Frankenstein must stop his creation before the monster's loneliness turns to violence.

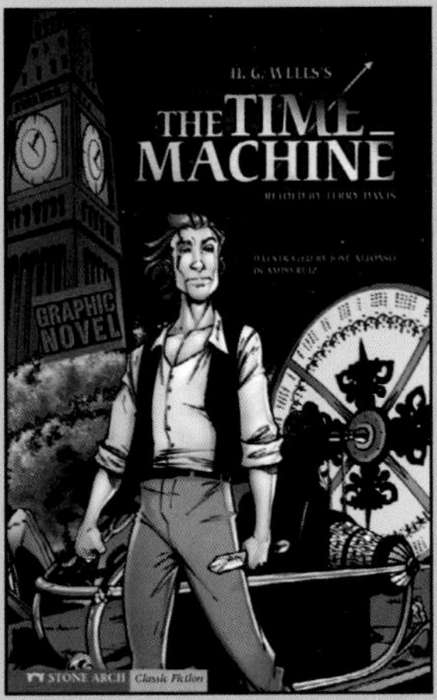
H. G. WELLS'S
THE TIME MACHINE
GRAPHIC NOVEL
STONE ARCH
Classic Fiction

The Time Machine

A young scientist invents a machine that he says will travel through time. His friends, however, laugh at the idea. To prove his Time Machine works, the scientist sets out into the distant future. Moments later, he crashes in a strange land inhabited by a group called the Eloi. Though he becomes friends with an Eloi named Weena, the Time Traveler soon fights for his life against evil Morlock creatures. Even worse, his Time Machine and only chance to escape, rests deep in the Morlock cavern.

INTERNET SITES

Do you want to know more about subjects related to this book? Or are you interested in learning about other topics? Then check out FactHound, a fun, easy way to find Internet sites.

Our investigative staff has already sniffed out great sites for you!

Here's how to use FactHound:

1. Visit *www.facthound.com*

2. Select your grade level.

3. To learn more about subjects related to this book, type in the book's ISBN number: 1598898310.

4. Click the Fetch It button.

FactHound will fetch the best Internet sites for you!